"Please, Tassie?"

I look at my pink low-top Converse, then at him, and back to the shoes. "Give me one good reason why I should help you?" Because I really, really need one. Especially since I feel like a complete moron for actually wanting to help him. It's like I can't resist rescuing the stray puppy who's bitten me a thousand times.

"We'd be helping each other," he explains. "I need a much cheaper place to live and you want to get into the Tri-Kapps."

"Ah!" I say, holding up my index finger. "But do I want it badly enough to let everyone think you've taken my pristine chariot out for its maiden voyage?"

"Your…chariot?"

"What would you like me to call it? My vaginal membrane? My cherry? My flower of purity? The winner's ribbon for my hump-day race?"

His handsome face contorts. "Chariot works."

"Great. And you're still not riding it."

"I didn't ask to. It's just something we'll let people think so I get the points. In exchange, for the next few weeks, I'll dote when we're around your uptight, intellectual elitist sorority sisters. And then you dump me. Simple."

I give it some thought—what it would mean to allow the blemish on my reputation.

"Come on, Tass. You know this is the best option for us both. Paweeeze?"

I look at Hunter, who has giant blue, anime-saucer eyes and a lower lip that's pouting for its life.

"No." I shake my finger at him. "Not the puppy face, Hunter."

He tugs on the hem of my T-shirt, his lower lip quivering. "Tassie..."

"Ugh. You are so juvenile. You know that, right?"

His face returns to its normal, annoyingly handsome perfection. "Yes. And thank you. You're making the right choice."

"Wait. I didn't agree to—"

He leans down and plants a big wet, closed-mouth kiss on my lips.

OTHER WORKS BY MIMI JEAN PAMFILOFF

COMING SOON!
Oh, Henry (Book 2, The Ohellno Series)
Mr. Rook (Book 1, Mr. Rook's Island)
Pawn (Book 2, Mr. Rook's Island)
Skinny Pants
(Book 3, The Happy Pants Café Series)
The Goddess of Forgetfulness
(Book 4, Immortal Matchmakers)

THE FATE BOOK SERIES
(Standalones/New Adult Suspense/Humor)
Fate Book
Fate Book Two

THE FUGLY SERIES
(Standalone/Contemporary Romance)
fugly
it's a fugly life

THE HAPPY PANTS SERIES
(Standalones/Romantic Comedy)
The Happy Pants Café (Prequel)
Tailored for Trouble (Book 1)
Leather Pants (Book 2)

SMART TASS

THE OHELLNO SERIES
BOOK ONE

MIMI JEAN PAMFILOFF

A Mimi Boutique Novel

Cover Design by Earthly Charms (www.earthlycharms.com)
Creative Editing by Latoya C. Smith (lcsliterary.com)
Line Editing and Proof Reading by Pauline Nolet (www.paulinenolet.com)
Formatting by bbebooksthailand.com

SMART TASS

CHAPTER ONE

"Jesus, Hunter. You're a bigger piece of shit than I thought," I snap, standing in the middle of the library at Austin U, with the star quarterback kneeling in front of me, his beefy arms wrapped around my legs.

What is he even asking for? Because he hasn't said and I don't know.

"I'm not leaving until you say yes, Tass," he mumbles with his head pressed into my kneecaps. Okay, really his mouth is wedged between my thighs—*not cool!*—so I just pretend we're engaging in kneecap contact.

"Come on, Tassie. It's just one little yes, and I'm gone." His sky-blue eyes gaze up at me with the sincerity of a blow-up doll while the student body chuckles and snaps off pictures.

Wonderful. Let's make a historical record of this mortifying moment.

"Get off me, Hunt! I have to get to class."

He tightens his iron grip, biting down on a shit-eating grin. "Not until you say yeeees," he sings.

I have no clue what he wants, but God, I loathe jocks. I hate the way they laugh at each other's douche-bag jokes. I hate how they strut around like they're God's gift to the universe herself. I hate their obsessions with cheap beer, pickup trucks, and blonde girls in short skirts.

And I especially hate this guy, Hunter Johnson. Aka Hunt. Also referred to by himself and his followers as "The Hunt," "The Man," "Mr. Amaze-football," and my own creation, "Dickhead." Okay. Mine isn't so original, but neither is the dipshit hugging my knees for no other reason than after all these years, he still hopes he'll get a rise out of me. But I wouldn't queef in Hunt's general direction to save his life. Not that I've ever queefed. Or had sex. Or…anything. But, hey, I have my "better than you" scoreboard. Hunt – 1. Tassie – 562.

And just why is my score so high? This game has been going on for as long as I can remember, starting in preschool all the way through high school. Hunter and I were neighbors. Technically, we still are since our parents continue living next door to each other back home.

Lucky me. But imagine my delight when I learned that Hunter and I would be going to the same university.

Both on full scholarships.

Unbelievable. I worked my entire life for straight As. I made sacrifices—mostly to my social life and girlish figure since studying didn't leave room for much else. Hunt, on the other hand, just threw around a ball while wearing tight pants and humping his way through the cheerleading squad.

Fed up with his little game, I reach down and grab a fistful of Hunter's dark brown hair that skirts his annoyingly strong jawline. His hair is longer than he used to wear it back in high school, and it's surprisingly soft, too. *I can make nice earmuffs out of it after I scalp him.*

"Ow! Hey," he squawks, but goes right back to locking up my legs the second I release his silky hair.

"All right," I say through clenched teeth. "What do you want, Hunt?"

"Say yes. That's all. Please, Tass?" His callused fingers press into my bare calves underneath my floral, knee-length skirt. Strangely, his hands feel satisfyingly rough.

What? No. You are not enjoying this.

Hunter's thumbs make tiny circles behind my knees, almost like he's heard my thoughts and agrees with them: *"Yeah, giiiiirl! You know it."*

A silent cringe tears through me.

"Dammit, Hunter," I say, doing a wiggle-step, trying to keep my balance. I'd prefer not to fall over and show the world my Hello Kitty Friday underwear beneath my skirt. "Get off!"

"Would love to." He laughs, wiggling his dark eyebrows. "My place or yours?"

"Har, har, asshole," I say.

"Ouch. Such words, little Tassie." He chuckles

and his breath tickles my inner thighs. It feels oddly intimate, and I don't like it one little bit. "Now, you really have to say yes."

"Yes to *what?* Use your words, tiny man." Tiny refers to his brain, not his body. In the size department, he's a tall, lean, mean football machine. A complete waste of a nice male body.

"I need your help." He makes a pouty face that quickly turns into—

"Nooo. Don't you do it! I'm so not in the mood. Don't you dare use the—"

"Paweeez, Tassie…" His blue eyes are super big and the tip of his pink tongue darts out the side of his mouth.

Oh God. Not the puppy face. I refrain from cracking a smile. He first used it on me when we were five to wheedle a graham cracker. Over the years, he's used it to convince me to do things like lie to his parents—"Yes, Hunt was with me, studying"— or to tutor him with algebra when he was failing. I never understood why I helped him because the guy made my life a living hell. *It's totally the puppy face.* Case in point, it still gives me the uncontrollable urge to laugh. It's just that stupid.

"Hunter, I swear you're the biggest…" Trying not to smile, I notice a few of his football buddies doubled over, cracking their shit up behind a row of books.

My smile vanishes like a wisp of steam over morning coffee—fair trade, French roast—in case you're wondering what I'm imagining dumping over his head at this very moment.

"You bastard," I curse under my breath. "This is some sort of dare, and you're still living in high school. Well, here's a blast from the past!" I manage a small jab-kick just above his knee, which creates enough space for me to land a real kick into his rib and—*ouch! My foot!*—rock-hard abs.

"Tass." He laughs, releasing me and rolling on his side. "Come on…"

There is no justice in this world. Not for women like me who reject this form of juvenile henpecking, just like I reject push-up bras, oppressive dictatorships, and football—okay, basically any sport that pays its athletes millions of dollars while people go hungry. Intelligence is the only currency that matters.

And Hunter Johnson is dumbass broke!

Okay, right about now you're probably asking yourself if I'm one of those nerdy girls who had a crush on the quarterback back in high school and got her heart decimated every time she saw him walking down the hall, because he didn't actually see her.

Oh hell no.

My father is a software engineer who's created six different algorithms to track global-warming patterns, my mother is an award-winning bioengineer working on a cure for cancer—I want to be her someday—and my brother is a tech CEO and millionaire at the ripe old age of twenty-nine. Don't even get me started on my aunts, uncles, and cousins—all doctors or scientists. With my 3.99 GPA and full scholarship to a university that is not Harvard, Yale, or Princeton, I'm the black sheep of the Summerset clan. But for better or worse, that's my family, and I love them. Even if their standards are incredibly high. Either way, there is zero, and I mean *zero* interest in sports or men of sports on my part.

Hunter especially.

So exactly what *is* the rub between me and him? I'll have to get to that later, because right now, I need to flee from this giant, six-foot-two turd who's determined to latch onto my crotch zone and embarrassed the hell out of me.

I push my glasses back up my nose and head quickly for the exit, praying that no one in my chemistry club has witnessed the altercation, but knowing the library is their turf and the chances of this moment not coming up at tomorrow's study group are nil.

"Great. Just great," I mumble to myself and throw my weight into the heavy steel door to go outside.

"I just want to fuck you, Tass! I need a virgin!" Hunt yells out.

A gust of hot sticky September air flows over me as I pause mid-step in the doorway, wondering if I've actually heard his words correctly.

No, the boy who beat the hell out of Kurt Lipmann in the eleventh grade, defending my honor, would not sink so low. But I'm not stupid, hard of hearing, or delusional. *Yep.* This cave-dwelling crustacean actually said what I think, and from the roaring laughter radiating inside the library, I know everyone else heard him, too.

Wow. Now I'm pissed.

I slowly turn to face my nemesis, who's standing with a gloating grin baked onto his piehole. He thinks he's got me. He thinks I'm going to lose it right here in front of all these people.

Not today, Huntie baby. My self-worth doesn't come from his approval or my sexual status. *I am a strong, smart woman.*

I take a deep breath, let it out, and return with a lifted chin and confident strides. "But Hunter, did your concussion-warped mind forget? You already fucked me. You did it to me in kindergarten and every year of my life since."

Ewwws! and *yucks* erupt from the theater of on-lookers. Yeah, I know I made it sound like he had sex with me when I was six. *Nasty!* And point for me. *Tassie – 566.*

I go on, using a sweet, calm voice to twist the knife, "So now that we've established you've achieved your perverted goal, I think you should consider fucking yourself next. In that giant asshole of yours. Oh, but wait. Your shrimp dick won't reach." I make a pouty face and hold up my pinky.

"Poor Hunter. But at least I'm technically still a virgin because of it, which allows me to be deflowered by a real man someday."

His cocky grin morphs into a flat pair of lips and twitching blue eyes.

He's pissed. Another point me.

I sigh contentedly, turn, and exit the library.

Brains beat brawn every time.

CHAPTER TWO

"Tassie, ohmygod. Where have you been?" my new dorm-roomie, Elle, nearly trips on her own two feet as she rushes toward me the moment I enter the bustling Kappa Kappa Kappa House for the wine-spritzer-Scrabble-thon. Tonight is a big to-do for us pledges because it's the last step in the process to become a member, and I've wanted to be a Tri-Kapp since I was a little girl. My mother was a Tri-Kapp, and so were two Nobel Prize winners along with a slew of famous scientists. They are the most well thought of female brains in the world and are invaluable to my future—job recommendations, career networking, and grants. So even though my mother belonged to the Yale chapter, this is my legacy, which is why I've taken special care this evening to look like a respectable Tri-Kapp. I have my dark hair pulled into a bun and have on sensible flats to go with my blue pantsuit. I even wore my thick-framed glasses to show everyone that I'm not afraid to fly my nerd flag high in the sky.

"I had some studying to do for chemistry," I tell

Elle, who is a honey blonde with a huge brain that rivals the gap between her front teeth. She has an IQ that's off the charts and is the likeliest person on the planet to solve world hunger. Tonight, she's wearing a black skirt and a blouse with formulas printed all over it. *Classy!* We're both science geeks, but she's majoring in physics, not bioengineering.

"Well," Elle says, "Lainey and Jessica were just asking about you. What happened in the library today?"

Lainey and Jessica are the Tri-Kapp leaders, so my pulse rate soars.

"It's nothing," I say. "Some stupid jock I knew in high school."

"Well, it's *not* nothing," Elle whispers just as I notice the other pledges glancing at me and smirking. "Everyone's saying you slept with that nauseating football guy."

My jaw unhinges, knowing that this could do me in. Tri-Kapps don't date football players. Ever. It's a long-standing, unwritten tradition. We hate them. They hate us.

Kind of silly.

"But that's not true," I hiss. "I was only trying to embarrass him so he'd stop—"

Elle pulls out her phone from her over-the-shoulder purse and shows me a video clip where I'm declaring to the world that Hunter Johnson and I "fucked."

Oh God. I screwed myself on this one. Deduct Tas-

sie point. Award to Hunter.

The clanking of a spoon against a wineglass chimes through the air, silencing the group of pledges. It's Lainey, president of the Tri-Kapps. She's wearing her frizzy blonde hair in a ponytail and has on a blue blouse with giant homemade Scrabble pieces safety pinned to the front. The letters spell out G-E-N-I-U-S.

"Good evening, ladies," she says as everyone—sorority sisters and pledges alike—turn to face her in the foyer that reminds me of something from *Gone With the Wind* with its grand staircase. "Welcome to the big night. I hope you've been reading your dictionaries because tonight is going to be prodigious!"

She explains the rules for the competition. Each pledge is to drink one wine spritzer before each round of Scrabble. The pledges will play each other, one on one, until there are ten people left, essentially cutting the group down from forty.

She continues, "Now, as you know, if you're here tonight, it's because you were *asked t*o pledge. Your GPA meets our minimum requirements and/or you're legacy with an impressive IQ. But," she wags her finger, "Tri-Kappas must be able to think on their feet and show they have commitment. So let's make some words, and may the biggest brains win!"

I want to roll my eyes at the whole thing because plenty of intelligent people aren't very good at this game; however, tonight isn't really about words. It's about winning. They only want smart women who are driven and competitive.

"I'm so nervous," Elle says as we line up for our first dose of watery chardonnay.

I shrug. "My parents prohibited television in the house, so we played Scrabble a lot growing up."

"Tassie? May we speak with you in the other room?"

Elle and I turn to see Lainey in her blue Scrabble shirt, standing with her sidekick, Jessica, both staring down their noses at me.

I paste on a polite smile, but the uneasy flutter in my stomach tells me this isn't good. "Uh...sure."

With all eyes on us, Lainey gestures for me to follow her into the living room, where the blue and white striped couches are pushed against the wall and small Scrabble stations are set up on TV-dinner trays. We go into the corner near a fake tree with pictures of the Tri-Kapps pinned to the leaves.

"Tassie, we're afraid we have to ask you to remove yourself from the running." Lainey flips her blonde ponytail over her shoulder and crosses her scrawny arms. Jessica, the sorority VP and her evil twin—only brunette and shorter—follows suit.

My heart makes a sad wave action. "Do you mind sharing why?" My brain is finding it difficult to come up with a valid reason. I've passed every pledge task with flying colors this last week, not that it even matters because I'm legacy.

"We hold ourselves to a high standard, Tass. And given what we've seen, you're simply not Tri-Kappa material. But I'm sure the Gamma Nus will take you."

Gamma Nus? That's the cheerleader sorority. Their only requirements to get in are to be pretty and pretty horny for football players.

This can't be happening.

"I don't know what you've heard," I say, "but I promise I have no interest in the Gammas or their meathead boyfriends."

"That's not what we saw in the library. We were there?" Jessica sings like a question, so it sounds like she's really saying "dumbass."

"Okay. Wait. That thing today was just some immature practical joke—"

"Looked like you were enjoying it," Lainey adds.

"Enjoying it? I don't think so. Actually, I take that back. I did enjoy it. I like sticking up for myself and not letting some gorilla in a human suit think he can humiliate me in public."

"Then what was with all that smiling and blushing?" she says, her voice filled with pomposity.

"Well, he and I—we," I stammer, wanting to make sure I explain this correctly, "we grew up next door to each other, but I assure you, Hunter Johnson has been the bane of my existence since I was six. I hate the guy." Yes, there were moments when he didn't behave like a complete asshole, but mostly he just tormented me. The torture ranged from egging my window once a month and TPing my house (Hunt always denied involvement, of course, but I knew), to calling me names and throwing half-eaten sandwiches at our "geek table" during lunch. And I really couldn't count how many times one of his cheerleader girlfriends snubbed me in the locker room because my body isn't worthy of *Playboy Magazine.*

"You hate him. Really now?" Jessica asks with a smirk.

"Yes. Hate. The guy is so stupid, he can't even tie his shoe without looking it up on YouTube first." That's not exactly true, but this moment calls for hyperbole.

I wait for Lainey and Jessica to see the light, but they simply stand there staring with disapproval Scrabbled on their faces.

Damn it, Hunt. I can't allow him to rob me of this.

"My mother was a Tri-Kapp," I say, hoping to salvage this situation. "My aunt was a Tri-Kapp. Every woman in my family has a PhD and an IQ over one forty. Do you really think I'm going to waste my time on a dumb jock who can't satisfy me in any way?" Because they can't begin to imagine the pressure I'm under to make something of myself and that includes picking a guy my entire family will approve of. I've never found anyone remotely qualified, and I won't make the mistake of bringing someone home who isn't one of us. My older brother made that mistake once. Just once. The girl broke up with him the next day because she said we'd intentionally marginalized her with our dinner conversation regarding gene mutation. We didn't do it on purpose. That's just the sort of stuff my family likes to talk about. Fitting in isn't easy. Not even for me.

Jessica shrugs. "Some girls are suckers for big muscles."

Now I cross *my* arms. They're being ridiculous to a point where I'm questioning wanting to be a Tri-Kapp, because a part of me—the grown-up part—can't help but shake my head at the immaturity of this conversation. It shouldn't matter who I date. I mean, weren't we all about empowering women and using our collective brainpower for the betterment of humanity? So to place a value on a woman based on the perceived quality of her man seems astoundingly backwards.

Not that Hunter is my man. I shudder at the thought.

I open my mouth to give these two elitist snobs a piece of my mind, but then I remember that I'm not doing this for myself. I'm doing it because it's expected of me. I'm a Summerset. Plus, there'd be the whole humiliation thing if I had to tell my parents I wasn't accepted into the Tri-Kapps. Legacies are practically given a free pass during rush week. All I need to do is win tonight's contest, something I've been training for since I could spell

W-I-N-N-I-N-G!

"Please," I say, opting for a bit of groveling, which feels extremely painful, "is there anything I can say to convince you to let me stay?"

Lainey's brown eyes are void of sympathy. "I'm sorry, Tass, but the Alphas nearly burned down our house last year in one of their many stupid pranks."

The Alpha Phis are the football fraternity that our lovely Hunter is very likely pledging, and they are the sworn enemies of the Tri-Kapps. As I've already stated, Greek rivalries are completely ridiculous, but they are also considered a time-honored tradition.

"And there was the break-in last night," Jessica adds, nudging Lainey. "Someone stole all of our calculators while we were out collecting trash for Save Our Parks Day."

I hold back a laugh. "The Alphas stole your calculators?"

"We don't know for sure, but who else?" Lainey says.

I can just see those ridiculous jocks getting hammered and coming up with the bright idea. *"Hey, dudes! Let's go break into the Tri-Kapp House, yeah, and steal their calculators. Har, har, har... Nerds won't know what hit them." Idiots. They're too stupid to live.*

"So you see," Lainey says, "we can't have our good reputation soiled by allowing that human trash to publicly humiliate one of our sisters simply because she has a jock hang-up. Or fetish. Or poor judgment—whatever you call that despicable display of neediness we witnessed this morning."

Wait. "How can you possibly interpret what happened in the library as me being needy?"

"Like I said, we were there." Lainey shrugs. "We saw everything, including how much you loved that silly little banter you had going on."

"That's because it's all she'll ever get from a guy like that," Jessica whispers loud enough for me to hear.

"It really was nauseating how much she wanted him," Lainey says to Jessica, as if I'm not even there.

My mouth gapes open. "The only thing I wanted was to kick him in his footballs!" I can't believe this. Hunter picks on me, and I get blamed for wanting him.

My gaze shuffles between Lainey and Jessica. This situation has reached maximum ridiculousness, and I'm feeling genuinely upset. Dare I say, outraged. They're so blinded by their hate for these Alpha guys that they're blowing up this morning's incident into a crazy witch hunt, the worst part being that I've just been demoted to lovesick nerdy puppy who'll take a beating merely to please Mr. Football.

"I am *not* some pathetic little thing who follows around the football captain from her old high school, letting him use her as his personal fun-time urinal cake..." *Great. Now I'm not making any sense either.* "I have way better taste in men."

The two stare with cocked eyebrows as if to say, *"Sorry. Not buying it."*

"Wow." I place my hands on my hips. Now the only thing I want is to prove how incredibly wrong and stupid these two are. Yes, my pride has been triggered, and I can't help but want to defend my honor and intelligence. Yes, I realize it's a sore spot for me, but everyone has them. Everyone. And mine is this: Being called stupid—directly or indirectly.

"You *think* I can't get a dumb guy like Hunter Johnson if I wanted? His only requirement is that you know how to giggle and you tell him how big his arms are."

About to speak, Lainey shakes her head. I know she's going to show me the door.

"Fine! I'll prove it," I say, cutting her off before she has a chance to end it before I've achieved vindication. And no. For the record, I will *not* be joining this fascist sorority.

An image of my frowning mother slaps me across the face. She's shaking her head of short brown hair, refusing to say a word as I break the news. I mean, not a week goes by without someone in my family—cousins, aunts and uncles included—announcing a mind-blowing achievement to share. "I was nominated for a Pulitzer for my work on irrigation." "NASA wants to know if I'll consider heading up their new project on thermodynamic rocket propulsion." Then there's me: "I couldn't get into a sorority because my neighbor made fun of me in the library."

Ugh! I have to get into the Tri-Kapps.

"Prove it?" Lainey laughs. "How?"

How. How? "I'll show you how easy it is to get a guy like him. Then I'll make *him* endure public humiliation."

Lainey and Jessica are no longer smiling as the room fills with pretty, preppy women awaiting further instructions, staring expectantly in our direction.

Lainey cracks a sadistic smile. "You can stay, Tass."

"What! No. Kick her out," whines Jessica. "She's a scummy Alpha slut."

Lainey holds up her hand to silence her minion. "She may play tonight." Lainey looks at me, glaring harshly. "If you survive the Scrabble-thon, you will get one week to show us we're wrong about you. But I want to see that Alpha boy groveling at your feet. We want to see him publicly decimated. Got it?"

I swallow down the lump of doubt gathering in my throat. I can do this, right? I mean, all I need to do is dress like I have an IQ of a baked potato and pretend my self-esteem is hinged upon getting a man's approval.

How hard can that be?

As for Hunt, I've endured thirteen years of his inane bullcrap. He's made my life a living hell. It wouldn't be completely unreasonable to teach him a lesson, one that's long overdue.

I look up at Lainey. I can practically taste victory already. "Got it."

She gives me the nod. "Off you go then. Table five. Let the games begin."

CHAPTER THREE

"You're not really going to do this, are you?" Elle asks the next evening, eyeing me over her history book, her back propped up against her headboard.

I swivel in the full-length mirror glued to the closet door on my side of the world's dreariest dorm room—gray carpets, white walls, brown furniture—that we've attempted to spruce up with a pink shag rug and a poster of Einstein wearing a tiara. I have purple floral-themed bedding and Elle has all orange. Yes, we love our girly things, despite what people say. Honestly, I think it's the number one stereotype I hear—smart girls are not feminine. That we don't like girly things or wear makeup or skirts or watch romantic movies. Not true. Some do. Some don't. Everyone's different. But it's never made sense to me that just because you dream of giving cold fusion to the masses or want to be the queen of terraforming on Mars, that you're instantly not a woman or can't be sexy?

Pig soap!

I completely embrace my femininity and hope

to work with my mother on her cure for cancer. That or a cure for jockism. There's probably a recessive caveman gene responsible for the unique combination of narcissism, dim wits, and large biceps.

"Yes, I am doing this," I say to Elle, checking out my pale legs. "Do you think I should get a spray tan tomorrow?" It's too late to take any action tonight because the party at the Alpha House started at seven. It's already eight, and I want to be sure to get there before Hunt's locked and loaded his hookup for the evening.

"You can't be serious?"

"Well, I'm not risking skin cancer simply to impress a guy." I hike up my black skirt so it hits mid-thigh. "I think I need something shorter that screams I'm easy."

"No. I meant this stupid bet with Lainey and Jessica." Elle sets her book in her lap, her brown eyes frowning in a way that reminds me of my mother.

"Why not? I passed the Scrabble test." *Can you say Q-U-I-X-O-T-R-Y for three hundred and sixty-five points?* "And they insulted my intelligence. Not to mention, I'm not allowing that meathead to ruin yet another stage of my life."

"Don't you think this is a little extreme?"

"Absolutely. But sometimes a girl's just gotta take a stand." And for this girl, it was about bleedin' time.

"What's the story with you and this guy anyway?"

"I really don't want to talk about it." I hate thinking about Hunter because once I start, I can't stop. There's too much baggage there.

She shrugs and props up her book on her lap. I can tell by her flat lips she's disappointed that I won't share. I also know she doesn't have many friends back home in her small town and she's a genuinely nice person. We actually requested each other as roommates through the online roomie finder. It helps match like-minded people so you don't end up with a person who's only into screwing and beer pong when you're trying to graduate with honors. Elle and I hit it off right away during our phone interview. She reminds me of Rachel, my best friend back home in The Woodlands, a suburb of Houston. Rachel got into Harvard. Yes, I am jealous. But more than anything, I miss her.

Which is why you need to make new friends.

I sigh, walk over to my bed across from Elle's, and take a seat. "Hunter Johnson is my neighbor who picked on me since the first day of school. He's partly to blame for my less than perfect GPA."

Elle lowers her book again. "What did he do?"

I fold my hands neatly in my lap. This is difficult to talk about because I'd promised myself that I would leave the past behind. Coming here to Austin U was supposed to be my fresh start.

I clear my throat. "The short version is that we

played together when we were little. Our mothers both worked and our fathers did, too, so Hunter and I went to the same daycare. Our parents helped each other out with carpooling and stuff. But then kindergarten started and so did his utter hate for me—the uncool nerdy girl."

Elle's round face crinkles up as if she were about to get a shot in the arm or something equally unpleasant. "I don't know if I want to hear this. Sounds too close to home."

I can't lie. It *was* pretty painful. That first day of kindergarten, my mom dropped us off. Hunter had on his Iron Man shirt, and I clung to my Harry Potter lunch pail. We walked in together, and I'd felt comforted having my best friend by my side in this new place. I remember standing there, taking in the big room with desks clustered together and lots of strange faces. Hunter simply walked up to a boy and jerked his head, as if to say "Hey, wassup?" Then they began playing. As for me, I was too shy to simply walk up to the other girls, who looked so pretty with their flashy barrettes and expensive shoes. I'd worn a plain tee, jeans, and sneakers. No frills. My mother didn't believe in all that, which could be the reason I like clothes so much as an adult. In any case, I felt more comfortable with Hunter—my friend—so I tried to join in on an awesome game of Lego car racing. Hunter took one look at me and said, "You can't play. You're a stupid girl."

I don't think I will ever forget the sting of his rejection—being shoved aside by someone I thought cared about me.

But life went on.

I made a few new friends—geeky like me—and Hunter and I still carpooled together since it was easiest for our moms. He kept to himself, playing with whatever portable video game thing his parents had bought him, me reading whatever book I was trying to master in the Magic Tree House realm. When we'd get to school, Hunt would always make sure to say something mean to me in front of his friends so everyone knew that while we rode in together, we were not friends.

Eventually, my mother caught on that Hunter and I were not "getting along," as she put it to his mom, who refused to discipline him or teach him manners. Years later, I'd come to realize that the poor lady was terribly shy and rarely spoke up to anyone, including her bossy rude husband, who worked in construction.

Anyway, the rest of Hunt's and my relationship was a blur. He followed his path—like a jock moth flying toward the glorious jock light, in search of fame, pussy, and glory. I followed my own path, working my butt off at school. When our paths crossed, almost daily, I was an object of ridicule. He would poke fun at my curly brown hair or make fun of my flat chest or math club T-shirts. "Hey, Tassie, lookin' fine in that little-boy body. Just when exactly are you going to hit puberty? My friends and I need to know 'cause we've got a bet going."

Asshat. I ignored him, of course, but it did little to deter the douche bag. I really think he got off on it.

But the strange thing was, during all those years, he never allowed anyone else to say a single word to me.

Not one.

If any of his stupid "bros" opened their mouths, they'd quickly receive the international bro-sign of shutthehellup: a punch in the arm. Hunter would then add a "Back off! Tassie is my nerd." Like he owned me in some strange version of reality that only existed in his head.

So twisted.

Then there was the day in the eleventh grade when Kurt Lipmann grabbed my ass in the hallway between classes. I yelled at the guy, told him he was a "feckless dick," and gave him a push. So many people were watching that I think he felt compelled to put me in my place—especially since he probably didn't know the meaning of feckless—so he slapped me. I wasn't having it. I went right after him with flying fists that did absolutely nothing except amuse the onlookers. Kurt and I were dragged apart and ended up in the principal's office. I got suspended for a day—for fighting and swearing—he got a full week. Justice had not been served in my mind. And, as it turned out, it hadn't been served in Hunter's mind either. He beat the crap out of Kurt the next week after school. Black eye, cut lip, the works. No, Kurt didn't tattle, but I knew. Why else would Kurt have come up to me at lunch, stared at his shoes, and said, "I'm really sorry, Tassie. It won't ever happen again." I remember looking across the lunchroom, where Hunter sat taller than the rest in his letterman's jacket, with his group of football cronies. His sky-blue eyes crackled with anger, almost like he was displeased for having to defend me.

Okay. What the hell? His actions left me feeling…well, I didn't know. Angry. Confused. I mean, I didn't need him sticking up for me. But the question begged, why would he? He lived to make me suffer.

That night, I went over to his house, and he answered the door in one of those tight tees he loved so much, likely because they showed off his bulging biceps and chest.

"Can we talk? Outside," I added.

Those sharp blue eyes, framed by a curtain of dark lashes, flashed a hard look. "What do you want, Tassie?"

I lifted a brow, stepped off his porch, and went to wait for him on his front lawn with my arms crossed. It was almost nine o'clock at night and dark out, but he was still likely worried about being seen with me, so I added, "I'm not leaving until we talk."

Hunter's broad shoulders rose steadily and then

fell with an impatient breath. He stepped out, closed the front door behind him, and walked over.

"What?" he said, all hostile.

"What the *hell* was that with Kurt?"

He shrugged. "What?"

"I know it was you."

"I don't know what you're talking about, Tassie." He flashed a cocky smile, like he was prouder than hell to have gotten away with it.

"Fine. Play that game. But I don't need you defending me, and I don't need you interfering in my life. In fact, isn't it about time you just leave me the hell alone?"

He chuckled. "We both know you'd miss me."

My jaw dropped. *What is the matter with him?* "Do you have any idea what you're doing to me?"

He stepped in so close I could feel the heat radiating off his tall frame. "No. What am I doing to you?" he said with his deep voice that always provoked a reaction in my stomach. The truth is that I loved the way it sounded, which completely infuriated me.

Being only five five, I had to crane back my neck to see his face and make sure he saw mine. "This isn't funny, Hunter. You're fucking up my life."

He jerked his head back as if shocked by that. "You're serious. You really want me to stop."

"Yes! An emphatic, astounding yes!" One would think after saying "leave me alone" five hundred times, as I'd done over the years, he'd get the picture.

A long moment passed, him staring into my eyes, the porchlight illuminating half his stupidly chiseled face, before he leaned down to whisper in my ear, "Sorry. But you're my nerd, Tassie."

I felt the heat of his breath on my ear, and it gave me goose bumps, though I was fairly sure they were the revolted kind.

"I'm not your anything, Hunt." I turned to leave, but he caught my wrist and snapped me back.

I sort of squeaked-yelped as my body slammed into him. "Hey!"

Hunter suddenly wrapped his big arms around me and...well, he gave me a hug. A big old bear hug.

What the hell? I stood with my body frozen like a block of ice. His large body felt warm and hard against mine, and he smelled really nice.

"Sorry that fucker hit you, Tassie," he said softly.

A million different things charged through my mind, but mostly I thought I'd bonked my head. Or an alternate universe had jumped out of the ground and sucked me in. Because Hunter Johnson went out of his coldhearted way to single me out and humiliate me almost daily. And now he had his arms wrapped around my body, being all protective and affectionate?

No. Nuh-uh. Something's not right.

I pushed him away. "Where do you get off…" I searched for the right words.

"Not with you. That's for sure," he said, with a snide little laugh.

My mouth fell open. *He's screwing with me. That's what this is.* Just another demented mind game.

"Just…fucking leave me alone," I spat and marched off toward my house. "I mean it!"

"Not a chance, Tassie!" he yelled. "I'd miss your dirty little nerd mouth too much."

And he'd meant it, too. After that, Hunter made sure to stop by my locker at least once a day— usually a drive-by to say something stupid like, "Lookin' mighty fine in those really big glasses, Tass." Or his all-time favorite, "Say it. Who's your favorite jock, my little nerd princess?"

To which I'd reply, "You're not my favorite anything. You're just an asshole."

"You know you love me."

"Like a crusty rash," I'd say.

"You don't get rashes—you belong to the awesome NBMs. Remember?"

Yeah, he liked throwing that one at me a lot. The "Not Before Marriage" group was my way of embracing my nerdiness. I wanted girls to see it was okay to wait. Sadly, there were only five in our group and one was a guy—Jeremy Flynn, who followed me around like a puppy until graduation day. Nice guy. Bad BO. Rachel, my best friend, was also part of the club.

Anyway, the daily banter between Hunter and me seemed to be the highlight of his pathetic, self-centered life until our senior year. He'd been away all summer at some stupid football camp, and when he returned, he'd changed. He stopped talking to me, teasing me, or looking at me. He didn't even beg for the occasional math help or alibi. He seemed...colder and distant. It was a little strange, but it was the best year of my life. College was ahead of me. High school would soon be behind me. The future was bright.

Until now. Hunter is ruining my life again.

"So?" Elle prods from her bed, the history book clutched to her chest. "Are you going to tell me what this football guy did to you?"

I look at my hands folded neatly in my lap and then back at her. I suddenly have zero desire to rehash the past.

"Nah, forget it." I stand up. "It's no big deal. We just weren't friends, that's all."

"Oh." She nods skeptically.

"So you feel like going to an Alpha party tonight?" I ask teasingly.

Elle's brown eyes bug open. "Uh...yeah. No. I have a brain, and those aren't welcome in the Alpha House."

"Point taken. How about loaning me a really slutty dress?"

She laughs. "Either you're insane or you have

gargantuan gonads, which, in either case, means you shouldn't be let out of this room."

"It's gonads," I say with a straight face. "I've been meaning to tell you, but I haven't been able to find the right time." I point to my crotch and then pretend I'm grabbing two round objects. "They're hairy. I mean, really hairy. It's gross."

"Ohmygod, Tass!" she says, shaking her head. "You're such a smartass."

"So I've been told." The question is, can I be a sexy-ass and seduce Hunter Johnson to win this bet?

CHAPTER FOUR

Yes. I am insane.

As I approach the Alpha House busting at the seams with partygoers and loud music, the reality of what I'm about to do hits me over the head like a lead balloon.

A) I am alone and going to a frat party. Hunter's frat party.

B) I am planning to catch Hunter with my womanly wiles to prove a point: that with my glorious brain, I can get any man I want, including the one guy Lainey and Jessica think I can't have but "need."

Yeah, because I'm sooo needy and all horny for those genius football players. So stupid. I hate those two chicks! Why the hell am I even here? I stop on the sidewalk just across the street from the two-story, wood-framed house with a large porch and black shutters. My heart is pounding a million beats per second, but not because I'm afraid of going inside alone. I'm afraid of failing. It's always about that with me, likely due to growing up with so many high achievers. I'd rather look like a jackass and win than fail and look like a loser. Failing means you aren't smart enough to figure out the right answer.

No. No. No. That's not right, I correct myself. *Failing is an essential element on the road to success.* Even in the lab, the failure of an experiment is equally as important as its success because it eliminates variables.

Yes, that's right. Tonight is like any other science project. I must not be nervous. I have set out with a hypothesis that dressing very sexy will attract a shallow man like Hunter—who I will thus refer to as "Evil Lab Rat" that only thinks with his penis. My clothing will tell evil Lab Rat that he and I are the same shallow species of creatures who only wish to fornicate.

Actually, since I'm here, I really should test out multiple variables.

I make a mental note of each test I will perform tonight, the goal being to determine which will prove more effective in getting Hunter—oops—Evil Lab Rat—to pursue the cheese.

Experiment #1: Appearance. I am wearing a short black skirt (that I've folded at the waist to make shorter), black heels (the only heels I own), and a low-cut red tank top (that I usually wear underneath a blouse). I've straightened my curly brown hair so it's as long as possible, and I have applied an obscene amount of makeup.

My second hypothesis is that giggling and acting

as if my brain is as useful as a paperclip will make Lab Rat feel smarter and therefore, will make him feel good. He will want to spend more time with me. *Experiment #2: Laugh at all his jokes and do not say anything remotely intelligent.*

My third hypothesis is that the Lab Rat is a complete narcissist and requires flattery on a regular basis for nourishment. *Experiment #3: Tell Lab Rat how big his muscles are.*

I take a moment to rehash my hypotheses, making sure I haven't missed anything. I haven't. My project is as simple as my subject.

I pull my mirror from my small over-the-shoulder purse, check my garish makeup—red lips, smoky eye shadow, and a pound of mascara. Without my glasses, I look the part. No brains. Just a nice college girl out for a dirty night of fun and hookups.

Let the experiment begin.

Right away, I decide that frat houses are gross. So is weed. It smells like skunk flatulence after the skunk has consumed a bad burrito. Surprisingly, however, the noxious potpourri fits the décor of this giant man-child dwelling. The living room, where I enter, has a pool table and is filled with crappy lawn furniture and a kiddy pool containing ice and beer. On the walls, posters of football players are graffitied with intellectual gems such as "pussy" or "big loser pussy." I assume these are people from the AU rival football team.

As I weave my way through the crowd, who's laughing and dancing and holding red cups or beer bottles, the hip-hop music hammers away in the background. *Ick. What noise pollution.* I much prefer thought-provoking songs made with actual instruments in there somewhere, like Ed Sheeran. Also, screaming profanity is only acceptable when I do it, and I only do it because it used to make me feel normal. *Normal-er.* Now I only do it because I feel it more accurately expresses my emotion. This is another misnomer I frequently see in movies or hear people say about highly intelligent people; that we are robotic and Spock like or that we all speak like Cambridge professors from the 1800s. Not necessarily untrue. Some of the smartest people I've met—triple doctorate colleagues of my mother and father, for example—are some of the most laid-back, slang-slinging, sloppy hipsters on the planet. Just looking at them, you'd think they worked at the local coffee house or smoked weed all day in their campers. But that's because they feel no need to impress others with their genius. They're too good for energy-sucking pretenses, because life is all about their work. Everything else can suck it. The point is, the old days of robot-nerd are long gone, so I never judge a book by its cover or use of f-bombs. Though, I do judge people who insist on making fart jokes (a minus) or wearing irreverent Game of Thrones "I brake for dragons" T-shirts (a plus). That's fair game.

I smile politely at the people as I bump my way through the crowd and snag an empty red cup to look more the part of party girl, although no one seems to notice me. This is good. I'm blending right in with all the perky blondes in short skirts— Gamma Nus and muscle heads.

"Hey there. What's your name?" says a deep voice just as a big body blocks my way to the kitchen.

Slowly, my eyes move up this...this...tree trunk. I'm talking great oak. Sequoia redwood. He can't weigh less than two seventy. With his height and size, he'd make a ripped guy like Hunter seem more like an anemic string bean.

I swallow down the dry glob in my throat. "Huh-huh-hi there?"

"You Gamma Nu, baby? 'Cause I'd like to Nu you."

I crinkle my nose at his pathetic attempt at wit. I'm about to tell him he should stick to football because speaking isn't going to get him far in life, when my real objective taps my shoulder: *Snag Hunter.*

Now, this guy isn't Hunter, but more rats equals more data. *Experiment #1 is successful. Slutty look has done the job. Move to #2: Laugh at his jokes and do not say anything remotely intelligent.*

I throw back my head and laugh. "You're cute." I poke his chest. "What's your name?"

"Henry."

"Hehe." I chuckle awkwardly. "Henry. Like, as in the second or the eighth?" *Uh-oh, was that nerdy?* I think it was since it requires some knowledge of history.

His smile drops. "What's the difference?"

Yep. I botched it. I have to say something stupid to cover my error so I go with, "One was a land-whore and the other a man-whore. Which are you?" I giggle in an attempt to flirt and show him how ignorant I am.

Henry's brow lifts. "Exactly how high are you?"

"What?" My jaw drops. "I am not stone—"

"Tassie!" a deep voice booms from behind me.

I know that voice. It's the reason I'm here. I pull back on my urge to panic and put on my game face.

Slowly, I turn in my very high heels, with one hand on my hip, and jerk my head. "Hey there, Hunt. What's up?" I immediately notice he's wearing a light blue T-shirt that makes his eyes stand out. His shorts—some cargo things—aren't anything special, but his legs are.

Wow. He could crack coconuts with those calves.

Hunter's intense eyes make a slow journey south before heading back north to my face. I wait for a positive reaction of some sort, but only get a snarl. A very disappointing result.

"What are you doing here, Tass?"

"It's rush week. Just out for a little fun." I shrug and bat my eyelashes, refusing to give up.

His nostrils flare. "You? Fun?"

"Why else would I be here?" *Experiment #3. Muscle flattery.* "Wow." I step closer and reach for a big bicep. "Have your muscles gotten bigger?"

He jerks his arm from my grip. "What are you doing, Tass?"

"Me?" I say innocently and point to myself, ensuring my index finger lands smack dab in the center of my cleavage.

Hunter takes the bait and looks at my womanly hilltops—really more like speed bumps—and then makes a *harrumph!*

"Outside. Now." He grabs me by the arm.

"Hehehe." I giggle stupidly, trying to maintain my cover in front of the onlookers. "Sure, Hunt."

He shakes his head and drags me through the hallway, into the kitchen and out to the back porch, where he pulls me aside, out of earshot from the pack of smokers.

"Tass, what the fuck is this?"

"I don't know what you mean," I say with a giggly voice that's slightly higher than my own.

His hands wave up and down my body. "This. And stop giggling. You sound like a stoned chipmunk."

"Silly. Chipmunks don't get high." I giggle again and then poke my cheek in deep, deep airhead contemplation. "Or do they?"

Hunter shakes his head, and his dark hair falls over his eyes. I sort of want to reach out and fix it— I mean, the guy's hair *is* soft—but I keep my hands to my sides. "Wow. You never change, Tass. Still playing dumb."

"Still?" To my knowledge this is a completely new approach to life.

"Okay, Alvin," he says with a long breath. "If you really want to play games, be my guest."

I'm not entirely sure what he's talking about, so I simply chalk it up to his testosterone-saturated mind. "For the record, I'd be Simon—not Alvin— note the glasses." I point to my face, and Hunter raises two dark brows.

Idiot me. "Glasses that I normally wear. But are not tonight. Because I have in contacts. Which I'm fully aware of because I put them in."

He continues staring with an expression ranging between utter disgust and irritation, which is clearly not the desired outcome given my goal of wanting to seduce him. For the sake of my future, of course. Because it would be silly to want him for real just because he's all built and big and has that deep voice.

A warm shiver ripples down my spine. *What? No. Not going there.* Shivers mean nothing.

"Look, Hunter baby," I say in a sugary-sweet voice, determined to get back on track, "I'm just a college girl, free from parental restrictions for the first time in her life, looking to have some fun." I bat my eyelashes. "Because fun is awesome. And I need me some."

God, I sound so ridiculous.

"Fun. Right. Just make sure you tell the Tri-Kapps that sending a spy here will only provoke a retaliation from the guys."

I huff. "Tri-Kapps? They don't have anything to do with me being here."

"Have fun at the party, Tassie." He heads inside, leaving me on the porch.

Dang. That went like crap. But I'm not giving up. I've come here on a mission, and as I've already said, I would rather make a jackass out of myself and win than go home a loser. So if my hypothesis on how to attract my Evil Lab Rat is incorrect, then I must go back inside and observe the animal in its natural habitat so I can formulate a new plan. Plus, I've never been to a real party, so I'm pretty curious to see what happens. Do people really swing from chandeliers, drink from beer bongs, and have sex in closets?

I shrug to myself and return inside with my mental pencil sharpened, ready to take notes. I will win this challenge. And I will make Lainey and Jessica eat their words.

CHAPTER FIVE

"So how'd it go last night?" Elle says as she comes into our room, where I've been since eight this morning, trying to decipher last night's data.

I take a sip of coffee that I've prepared in the microwave by boiling water in a glass measuring cup and then carefully pouring it into my Melitta filtering system. I cannot compromise when it comes to my vices, and good coffee feeds my dark side. After all, I have no sex life because school is my boyfriend and science is my lover. They are demanding, and between the two, they leave little room for anything but coffee. And occasionally shaving my legs. And shopping online late at night when my brain won't rest. But coffee is definitely the all-star.

Jesus, did I just think "all-star"? One night at the Alpha House has resulted in my using jock lingo.

"I think I have a jock-over," I mutter at my notebook, sitting at my desk, which is pushed against the foot of the bed just like Elle's.

"You got drunk?" Elle drops her red backpack

and plops onto her orange bed.

"No. But I spent so much time listening to Alphas talk about 'the game, dude,'" I say in a deep dopey voice, "that it gave me a headache."

"And what about Hunter? Any luck?"

"Nope. And I'm at a complete loss." Basically, he ignored me all night, though I did catch him giving me side glances every time I spoke to one of his frat brothers. It was like he couldn't help keeping an eye on me, but at the same time, he didn't look worried one bit. "The weird part was that I saw girls hitting on him all night, but he wouldn't give them the time of day. He stuck to his beer and playing pool."

"Hmmm…" Elle wiggles her puckered lips from side to side. "Maybe he's not into girls?"

I give that some thought. "Not likely. I mean, it's possible, but he literally whored his way through high school." *Leave no pussy untouched!* That was Hunter's and his friend's lame-ass motto.

"So he's probably not gay, and he showed no interest in you or any other girl. Hmmm…" She scratches the side of her head. "Maybe he's in love."

"What?" I whip up my head, but my heart tumbles onto the floor and twitches in agony. *It can't be. It can't be. Yet…* "Oh my God. Maybe you're right." It's the only explanation that fits.

I hang my head. "I'm screwed." Yet it somehow bothers me more that Hunter has found love. Because…because… Well, I don't really know why.

I suppose because he doesn't deserve it. Not when he ruined my social life and any chances of experiencing romance during my teen years. No guy would dare come near me, besides BO Jeremy, for fear of being picked on, too. Nerd by association. *I haven't even been kissed. Not once.* And it's worse than that movie.

"Well," says Elle, grabbing her backpack and fishing through its contents, "I don't think you would've succeeded anyway. He already knows you're smart, and he's not into smart girls. None of those guys are."

I bob my head. "You're probably right." It was silly to think I could put on an act and convince Hunter that I'm some airhead bimbo. He knows me too well. And despite my hate for him, he's not *that* stupid. I tutored him enough times to know he has a brain, but chooses to use it sparingly. He had no issue understanding algebraic formulas when he focused hard. That's what always baffled me. He could've done better. He could've had good grades, but he chose to act like a dumb jock simply to fit in.

"Well." I sigh. "At least I learned what that big scene at the library was all about."

Elle pauses the search at the bottom of her backpack. "And?"

"I heard a bunch of the guys talking about some stupid scavenger hunt they have going for rush week. The guys with the top twenty points get in."

"Seriously?"

"Yep. I snuck upstairs and found the scoreboard in one of the bedrooms. Did you know that breaking into the Tri-Kapp House and stealing their calculators was only worth two points?" Seems so little when they could've gotten arrested.

"What morons. How much was sleeping with you worth?"

"Oh. That. It was worth ten points, but the task was to get me to agree. Well, not me, exactly. It was 'Get green light from virgin. Witnesses required. Penetration optional.' Can you believe that?" I shake my head. "So disgusting."

Elle shrugs like she's simply not surprised. I suppose I'm not either.

"The irony is that Hunter's twenty points away from the top twenty," I add. "Looks like he's not getting in."

"Seems like a nice way to blackmail him," she mumbles absentmindedly, pulling out a pack of gum.

"Wait. What did you say?"

"What?" She opens the little box and holds it out, offering a piece.

"No, thanks. Clashes with my coffee." I flash a quick smile. "Can you repeat that part about the blackmail?"

"Oh. That. Well, not that I advocate cheating, but if you were the cheating sort, it would only make sense for the two of you to enter into secret squirrel—that's military lingo for an agreement on the down-low. Spy stuff."

I lift a brow.

"Oh, I've been reading spy novels lately. I like guessing the endings."

"You have time to read?" Because I don't. I barely have enough time to sleep.

"Sure. Can't spend your whole day studying."

I growl at her. "Must suck to be so smart."

"It does, actually. Nothing makes you feel lonelier than knowing only a handful of people on the planet have the capacity to understand you completely."

"Because everyone else is too dumb?" I ask.

She nods.

Ouch. "Exactly how smart are you?"

"One sixty."

"Seriously?" I'm a dunce compared to her, and I scored one forty-one last time I checked. That's near genius, but not quite. Which reminds me, I should get tested again. For me, IQ tests are kind of like checking my credit score. Gotta do it at least once a year to remind me that I'm sexy in my own brainy kind of way. Sort of like when a hot girl looks in the mirror and says, "Yeah, I'm prettier than the rest. That's why everyone hates me."

Of course, IQ is not the same as being educated. IQ measures the ability to learn, comprehend, and problem solve. Education is the process of acquiring knowledge. These are two separate things, although not entirely unrelated. For example, a person with a superior IQ learns at a faster pace, thus can acquire knowledge faster. However, a person with a superior education can easily outsmart someone with a genius IQ who's lacking knowledge. Okay. I'm rambling. My apologies.

I inhale deeply. "Not to insult you, my genius goddess, but if you're a one sixty, why are you here?"

She pops a piece of gum in her mouth and chews. "You're smart, too. You tell me."

"Umm…" I like puzzles, so I take a moment to figure it out. "You're secretly working with the CIA, studying the common folk, and coming up with a weapon of mass destruction?"

"Yes." She gives her index finger a shake. "I'm an evil genius."

"Okay, smarty-pants. Why are you here?"

"Honestly? I didn't want to be far from home. My parents are only a two-hour drive away."

"That's so sweet."

Her expression wilts into something melancholy. "My mother has in inoperable brain tumor. My sister is only ten minutes from their house, but I want to spend as much time as I can at home."

Oh no. So this is why Elle said she'd be staying at her parents' on weekends. And it breaks my heart to hear it. I literally want to cry. I cannot stand thinking of losing anyone, let alone watching my mother die.

"I'm so sorry, Elle. Are you okay?"

"Meh. As good as can be expected, but that's why I wanted to room with you. I read your bio on the roommate finder site."

My bio said that my one goal was to eradicate cancer, and I meant it. I can't imagine doing anything else with my life, and maybe it's because I grew up listening to all the painful stories from my mother. People she couldn't help. Families destroyed. All I know is that it feels like a war, and I want to fight.

"I'm sorry that your mom is sick," I say quietly. "I wish I were smarter and could build a time machine to the future because I know we'll find a cure." I flash a comforting smile, wanting to relieve her pain in some small way, but know I can't.

She smiles sadly and takes a deep breath.

"If there's anything I can do to help you," I say, "anything at all. Just ask."

"Thank you. But you know what I'd really like?" She smiles pensively.

"What?"

"Food." Elle pops up from her bed and heads for the door. "Gotta get to the cafeteria before they close for lunch."

She's gone before I can offer to go with her, but it's probably for the best. She seems to want to be alone right now, and I'm guessing it's because that wasn't easy for her to open up, which I completely understand. Sharing private, emotional things makes me uncomfortable, too. I don't like feeling vulnerable. I don't like telling people things they can use to hurt me. Of course, this makes acquiring new friends a little difficult, but I've managed. I simply need a lot of time to warm up to people and trust them.

As I'm left sitting there with my thoughts, I look down at my notes and shake my head. *Hunter is in love.* The thought makes my stomach twist with uneasy emotions. It makes no sense that this would bother me so much. Well, other than the fact that if he's in love, he's not going to play ball with me and I'm not getting into the Tri-Kapps.

But this sensation in my gut feels bigger. It feels like anger.

All right, calm down. Maybe Elle is wrong. Hunter isn't boyfriend material—he can't even be loyal to one brand of beer. I know because I saw him drinking three different kinds last night. *Philanderer.* So could something else be going on with him?

My mind flashes back through that last year of high school when he seemed so different—still part of his social circle and playing football, but lacking his exuberant display of douchebaggery. Come to think of it, I can't recall him dating anyone either.

There's only one way to find out for certain what's going on with Hunter. I'm going to go see him and ask. Simple. Logical. It's the most efficient course of action, and I'm on the clock.

CHAPTER SIX

Dressed in cutoffs and a white T-shirt, I ring the doorbell at the Alpha House, ready to cut to the chase.

The door swings open and out pops a giant head. It's Henry, the enormous tree trunk from last night. Actually, now that I'm seeing him in the daylight, he sort of looks like a really big version of Liam Hemsworth, but with green eyes.

"Hi, I'm here to see Hunter."

He yawns and sniffles. "He's not here. Did you check his dorm?"

"You sound like you have a cold." I step back.

"Hangover."

"Hydration, hydration, hydration. Prevents your liver and bile production from frustration."

He gives me a look.

Oops. I've let my geek out of the box again. "I checked the dorms, but his roommate says he's always here."

"Hey, I recognize you from last night. You were that waaay stoned chick in the short skirt."

"No, you were drunk, as you've pointed out, which only made it seem as though I was under the influence. By the way, you know it's ridiculous to call yourself an athlete and be so unhealthy, right? Sooner or later, your bad habits will turn into addiction and then you'll just be another statistic, sitting in a secondhand La-Z-Boy, wearing a wifebeater, reminiscing about the good old days, and wondering why you have to always choose between a case of Pabst or fixing your crappy car so you can collect your unemployment check."

"You're still high, aren't you? Because I can't understand what you're sayin'."

No, of course you don't, you dumb jock. "Yes. I'm flying," I say to appease him and get on with the conversation.

"Thought so, man."

"And Hunter? Any idea where he'd be?" I ask.

"Try the football stadium. He's probably at practice."

"Thanks, Henry." I turn to leave.

"Wait. You're also the virgin from the library." Henry chuckles and yells over his shoulder, "Hey, guys! Look who's here for Hunter! The virgin!"

Oh, lord. I hang my head and scurry the hell out of there, but I can hear screaming inside the house. Something about getting the marker ready for some "ten-point action."

Jesus. I hate jocks.

Thankful for having worn my comfy pink, low-top Converse, I head back to the campus five blocks away. It's late in the afternoon, and the sticky heat makes my curls go wild. I give them a quick finger-comb, deciding it's better to embrace the beast rather than fight it. Normally, I wear it in a ponytail or braid or something to keep it caged.

As I hit the campus, it's relatively quiet at first, not unusual for a Sunday, but the moment I'm within earshot of the stadium, I hear cheering.

Strange. There aren't any games today. I'm sure of it. Otherwise there'd be thousands of fans crowding sidewalks and clogging the streets.

I enter the stadium through the side gate that leads straight to the bleachers. Immediately, I notice the cheerleading squad sitting down on the edge of the field, watching the team practice. All eyes seem to be on Hunter, or maybe it's just my imagination. After all, he does have the ball.

I watch as he makes a pass, but the cheerleaders—Gamma Nus—continue staring at him. *Nope. They're definitely watching Hunter.* The guy has his own freaking personal harem to cheer him on during practice.

For a moment, I'm kind of jealous. I mean…not because I want him. No, no. That's ridiculous. It's because, well, obviously I'm jealous of his harem. Who wouldn't want one? Mine would be cheering while I crank through chemistry formulations. And they'd be dudes. Hot dudes in khakis and Polos because that's how I like 'em. Built and preppy.

Down on the field, the coach blows the whistle and the players stop running around like uniformly dressed chickens. I don't like sports, so I know virtually nada about the rules. I just know the coach looks unhappy because he's making Hunter repeat the play.

"Hey, Hunt! Don't worry. We still love you!" screams one of the girls—a blonde sitting toward the middle of the pack of about twenty women.

Hunter seems focused on the ball and ignores her, but that doesn't deter her or the others from whistling or catcalling.

How rude. He's not a piece of meat. He's a human being.

Wait. What? I practically slap myself for having such a compassionate thought for the guy who's cost me so damned much that my life has been irrevocably damaged. Okay, yes. I know that I am partly to blame for allowing him to get to me, but I'm not Superwoman. I'm not impervious to public humiliation or ridicule, and considering what he put me through, I think I fared as well as anyone might. He never saw me sweat. I never gave him attention or took him seriously. Not really. Not as far as the world was concerned. My friends, parents and teachers never suspected that underneath my cool and indifferent exterior was a lot of pain.

I sometimes wondered if even Hunter knew.

Of course he did. How could he not? Asshole.

"Hey, Hunter! Show us those moves, baby!" screams another girl.

Hunter looks over at her and winks. He even flashes a little dimple.

Oh yeah, aren't you Mr. Charming with your ridiculous little fan club.

The players break into two groups and face each other to do that whole lining up and bending over thing. Just as a guy in the middle passes the football to Hunter, and Hunter is poised to throw, a surge of bitterness overtakes me. I stand up and scream, "Hey, shrimp dick! How about *not* missing this time?"

The ball hurtles right into his fan club, because Hunter's not looking where he's throwing. He's looking at me. Snarling.

The coach blows the whistle and everyone turns to glare in my direction.

Uh-oh. I smile awkwardly and make a little pump with my fist. "Go Pirates?"

"You! Out!" screams the coach.

I hold up my hands in the "I surrender" position and turn to leave before I get mobbed. *I can't believe I did that.* I stop. *Wait. I can't believe I just did that! It felt so damned good. Like...amazing.*

I smile and head down the bleachers, making my way to the gate.

"Hey! Tassie!" an angry voice calls from behind me.

I freeze, knowing I'm about to get an earful, but

I realize that I don't really care. For the first time, I'm not the one taking the hit and sucking it up. It feels fantastic.

I turn slowly and watch Hunter jogging toward me, removing his helmet.

"Hey, Hunter," I say in a sugary-sweet voice.

"What *the fuck* was that?" He stops two feet in front of me, frothing at the mouth.

I shrug. "Ummm…it's called payback. You like it? Because I've got more. In fact, I'm thinking from now on, I'll be at every game."

"What's the matter with you?"

"Are you in love?" *Huh, strange.* I wasn't expecting that question to come out, and I certainly don't know why I added the bitter tinge to my voice, making it sound like I'm accusing him of cheating on me.

He stares for a long moment. "What's going on with you, Tass? This is my fucking practice. You can't show up here and pull this shit."

"Oh no. Am I…*bothering* you?" I say in a snide tone.

"Yes. And you should go now."

"I was going. You're the one who came after me."

"Then-then don't come back," he says, all flustered. And I realize that I'm thoroughly enjoying being the aggressor for once. I like not being his doorstop, and I want more.

"Oh, I will." I smile and turn to continue on my

way. "You're my jock now, Hunter! Better get used to it!" I call out over my shoulder. I can feel his blue, blue eyes burning into the back of my head as I walk away.

Damn, I love this.

CHAPTER SEVEN

"Okay, Elle. New plan." I burst into our dorm room, feeling like the universe has offered me a new lease on life. It has never occurred to me to take action or revenge, but now that I realize Hunter—the celebrity star quarterback—is vulnerable, I can't wait to give him just a little taste of his own medicine. Just a little.

Elle pulls her earbuds out. "Sorry?"

"My new plan. Relentless heckling."

She crinkles her nose. "Did I miss the bus? Because you've obviously gone somewhere without me."

I close the door and plop down on my bed. "Did you know that Hunter bullied me for thirteen years?"

"Really?"

I nod. "Yes."

"Why did you put up with it?"

"I guess…" I shrug. "I think because letting him know he got to me would feel like letting him win." Once again, I'll point out that I'd rather look like an ass than lose. "So I ignored him, which only made him try harder. Or I would smile and tell him how ridiculously stupid he was." That usually pissed him off and provoked more incidents.

"Still. Thirteen years?"

I swipe my hand through the air. "I'm over it. But it's dawned on me that Hunter has never been an outcast or ridiculed."

"Your point?"

"I'm going to let him know that no bad deed goes unpunished."

Elle cocks her head. "Explain how this will allow you to win the bet with Lainey and Jessica to make him your boyfriend."

"It won't. Or maybe it will. He'll be begging for mercy and do anything I say after I make up a bunch of shrimp signs and pass them out at the next game. I'll tell everyone it's to intimidate the rivals, but Hunter will see them and unravel. It will completely mess with his head."

"You're serious."

"As a heart attack. On a cruise ship. That's forgotten to stock aspirin and defibrillators."

"Have you always been this crazy, or have you only just recently lost your mind?"

She thinks I'm crazy, but that's only because she doesn't know.

I cross my arms over my chest. "What if I told you that he once had the entire school wear white T-shirts to honor my virginity."

"That's pretty mean."

"Just the tip of the iceberg, but I think his most memorable prank was when he had everyone write me in as homecoming queen."

"What? Why?"

"He thought it would be hysterical to see me put on a frou-frou dress and ride in the town parade." Hunter planned to make me sit next to him and humiliate me—or something like that.

"So you were homecoming queen?" she asks, her eyes going wide like saucers.

"I rejected the title."

"I'm sorry." Elle blinks. "But can you go over that part again? Hunter persuaded everyone to vote for you so you would be homecoming queen?"

"Yes."

"And...was he voted homecoming king?"

"Yeah. So?"

She tilts her head to one side. "Is he a psychopath?"

"Not that I'm aware of."

"Brain damaged in any way?" she asks.

"Of course."

"Seriously." She gives me a look.

"Okay, no. He's not suffering from any brain damage that I'm aware of."

"Does he practice sadism or satanic rituals or is he a superfan of the movie *Carrie*?"

"No. Where are you going with this?" I ask.

"I like a mystery—it's my thing. And I'm very

proficient at guessing underlying motives and, therefore, the ending." She inhales deeply. "Don't you find it a tad peculiar that a non-sadist, non-brain damaged, non-psycho, non-*Carrie* fan would go to such lengths and make you homecoming queen just to harm you?"

"Not when it comes to Hunter. He's cruel. He once held me down in the fourth grade, gave me a noogie, and then spit a giant wad of gum in my hair." It took two jars of peanut butter to get it out.

"Ah. But did you see him lavish his 'cruel' attentions on anyone else in such a manner?" she asks.

"No, Sherlock Homes, but I don't see how that matters."

She shakes her head. "What's the first rule of kindergarten? When a boy teases a girl, it means he…?"

I frown. "Now you're off your rocker. He does not like me."

"I beg to differ. I think he was into you. Big time. The hypothesis fits, Tassie."

"No. It doesn't. And I'm going to ruin his life. He's going to know what it feels like to be laughed at." She had absolutely no clue what I went through. And no one in their right mind would claim his actions were motivated by love.

A booming knock on the door startles us from our debate. I turn and pull open the door, finding… "Hunter?"

He steps inside the room, smelling of sweat and

anger—whatever scent that is.

"What are you doing here?" I ask.

"I've been standing out in the hallway, and I just heard everything you said."

Oh boy. Not good. On the other hand, what do I have to be ashamed of? My feelings are just, and I've done nothing wrong.

"Leave," I say. "Before I…spank you." *Why did I say that?*

He ignores me and then turns to Elle. "Can you excuse us? Tassie and I need to have a little chat."

Elle bites her cheeks and pops up from her desk. "I'll go sharpen pencils in the library."

"Wait. You don't have to…" She's gone before I can finish my sentence.

I scowl up, up, up at Hunter's tall frame. "How dare you eavesdrop and then run her out."

"Well, you, me, and my shrimp dick need a little privacy."

"Little is right," I snarl.

"Doubtful." He starts reaching for the zipper of his uniform pants.

"Whoa! What are you doing?" I hold out my hands and close my eyes.

"Well, you're obviously obsessed with my cock, and I have nothing to hide, so here it is."

I can't help but peek, but his penis is still in his pants.

"Come on. You really think I'd show it to you?" He scoffs.

"Who knows what you're capable of? You're obsessed with tormenting me."

"Really? What the fuck was all that you just said to your roommate?"

"It's called justice, Hunter. Because making me lose my chance to get into the Tri-Kapp House was the last freaking straw."

"What are you talking about?"

I look at him, and his annoyingly vivid blue eyes. "Well, I'm not exactly out, but I will be because of you."

"What did I do?"

"What you always do," I bark. "You humiliate me and put me down, and that little display in the library on Friday was just the thing to convince them that I'm not good enough."

"Because...why?"

"They think our little hate war is a love war, me being the aggressor."

"I'm not following," he says.

"They hate you. They hate Alphas. They think I let you abuse me like that because I'm into you."

His gaze is empty at first, but then he breaks out into hysterical laughter. "Yeah. I fucking see that." He gulps down some air between laughs. "Hysterical."

Well, at least someone agrees with me. "Exactly."

"So what was your plan? To torture me with shrimp-dick signs so they'd see you as Tri-Kapp material and let you in?"

"Maybe, though my original plan was to get you to fall in lust with me so I could humiliate you somehow."

"That makes no sense."

He's right, but…"It made sense at the time. And it's no worse than your lame scavenger hunt, which you're losing, so ha!"

He takes a sudden interest in his tennis shoes. "So you heard about that."

"Yes, I did. And thanks to you and those morons, I won't be getting into my sorority. My mom really wanted this for me, Hunter, but here I am, yet again, having to disappoint her. Next, I'll be listening to another speech about how I'm not living up to expectations. Because of you! Do you understand how much pain you've caused me, how much damage you've done to my life? I mean elementary, middle school, high school—those weren't enough for you? Now you have to ruin college, too? What did I ever do to you?"

The words coming from my mouth help me realize just how crazy he makes me. It's a wound I've never overcome, which is likely the reason I've emotionally regressed back to high school.

He stares down at me for a moment, his expression undecipherable. I suppose if I had to guess, I'd say he looks confused.

"I, uh…gotta go." He turns for the door.

"Oh no. You're not running away from me, mister!" I dash to the door and slide between him and the exit. I'm realizing this has to end. It's doing bad, bad things to my maturity level.

"Move, Tassie."

"No. Not until you say you're sorry and you promise to leave me alone from now on."

He stares down at me, and I notice how the scruff along his strong jawline isn't dark like his head of shaggy silky hair. It's more of a red brown with black mixed in. I also notice how his bottom lip is kind of pouty and very sensual. I've never actually looked at his face before. I mean really, really looked at it—the way his dark brows arch over those intense blue eyes with thick black lashes, the high cheekbones and the slight indentation in the hollows of his cheeks or the angular jaw. In my mind, I always saw him as that little boy with the fat cheeks who broke my heart, but now I realize how he's grown into this...this man with a scruffy short beard and muscles and everything.

Okay. He's nice looking. So what if I never noticed? On the inside he has nothing to offer.

I suddenly realize he's sort of just standing there looking at me, too, and it shocks me like a gust of frigid winter air. He's staring at my lips. Really staring.

My heart suddenly kicks into high gear and adrenaline pumps through me. I don't like it one little bit. It's awkward and uncomfortable and my body is all hot and—

Sexually flustered? No. No, no, no.

I step to the side and look away, crossing my arms over my chest. "Go. Just go," I say.

From the corner of my eye, I can see him reach for the handle, but he doesn't turn it. I hear him breathing, almost an angry pant, like he wants to hit something or say something, but can't or won't.

He suddenly jerks open the door and disappears, not bothering to close it, leaving me just standing there, trying to digest the weirdness that just happened.

You just totally got hot for Hunter.

Fuck. I hang my head and give it a shake. *I think it's time I have sex.* My body clearly needs it.

CHAPTER EIGHT

That next night, I dream I am a Salem witch being dragged through the town square while the crowd throws rotten cabbage and undressed Barbies at me. Yes. Strange. Possibly symbolic of my fear of emotional exposure. That or I really dislike cabbage and naked Barbies. When the torch-wielding masses tie me to a post, I notice I'm standing atop a heap of obsolete electronics—Motorola flip-phones and Nokia bricks. I'm fairly sure there are a few pagers and fax machines buried underneath it all, too. Just beyond the mob, I see my parents' emotionless faces, and I scream for help, but they don't see me. Only the people with the torches want anything to do with me, and they want to watch me burn along with the other garbage that was once deemed smart and essential. They light the fire, and I yell, "Let me go! I am not obsolete!" Through the flames and smoke, I see someone fighting through the angry mob. Hunter's handsome face appears and our eyes meet. The look in his eyes tells me he wants to save me, but the people are pushing him back, screaming at him. The fire ignites my legs as he mouths *"I'm sorry."* I'm mortified to see him in so much pain. I don't want that for him.

The cell phone rings on my nightstand, jarring me from my strange but horrific dream. I grab the thing and look at the caller ID. It's not a number I know, but it's six in the morning and I should be getting up for my 7:30 a.m. class.

"Hello," I say, my voice all scratchy.

"Hey, Tass. It's Hunter," says that deep, deep voice I've come to loathe.

I blink and rub my face, wondering why the hell he's calling so early.

"We need to talk," he says. "I have practice right now and then class until two, but can we meet somewhere after?"

I scratch the top of my head. "I have chem lab until three."

"Fine. Meet me at my dorm room at 3:15."

"What's this about?" I ask.

"Best to talk in person."

"Okay. You're being mysterious and that makes me feel uncomfortable. You're not up to anything, are you?"

"No," he replies.

"Would you tell me if you were?"

"No. But I'm not."

Says you. "Wait. How did you get my number?"

"Your mom. I called her and asked for it."

"At six in the morning?" I ask.

"No. I called her the other day."

Now he's really piqued my curiosity. He'd been planning to call me? "Okay, see you at 3:15."

The day crawls by like a slug on crutches, and my mind can't help wondering what Hunter wants. Ten minutes before the end of chem lab, I catch myself doodling in my notebook:

Revenge.

Apology.

Censure.

These are my three hypotheses regarding Hunter's request to meet. He wants to subject me to some sort of public humiliation after the heckling episode or it's finally sunk into that thick pigskin-lined head of his that he's genuinely caused me pain. *Or…or…he wants to yell at me again.*

My mind darts to that brief moment just before he left my room—the way he made my heart thump inside my chest. The sweat on my palms. The body tingles.

I push the thought away, feeling more ridiculous than ever. My body is in its prime, and biology is demanding I pick up her phone call. You know, the call of procreation. "*Find strong male. Make babies. You know you want to.*" That's what really happened. My brain, hardwired with millions of years of evolutionary coding, doesn't care that I'm a modern woman with aspirations.

Ha! Well, lucky me, I'm smarter than my brain.

Wait. That doesn't make any sense. I let out a soft

groan as the professor calls it a day. The moment I stand, my stomach makes loop-de-loops and my heart goes crazy. *Holy crap.* I'm nervous. Really nervous.

I realize I can't go see Hunter. I don't want to. I want to run far away from him. Being outside my comfort zone makes me feel like I'm lost because I don't know what to do. And not knowing what to do will lead to failure. I'd rather die than fail because I've got a chip on my shoulder the size of the Arctic.

I take a deep breath. Whatever's going on with me—this out of controlness—can't be good. *I'll just have to call Hunt and tell him I'm busy. Or that I have the flu. Of my sanity.*

I throw my backpack over my shoulder and dig into my jeans pocket for my cell. I type in, *"Hey. Can't meet today. I'm sick."*

As I step outside the room and hit SEND, I hear a phone beep to my right in the hall.

Hunter's standing there holding his phone and glaring at me.

"Oh. You…you're here." *Dammit!*

"I had a feeling you'd flake."

"I'm that predictable?" I ask, kind of surprised he knows me so well.

"I figured after your little chew-out yesterday that you might get second thoughts about meeting. That, and now I know you don't trust me. Not even a little."

"You're a lot smarter than you look."

"You're funny," he says dryly and jerks his head toward the exit down the hall. "Let's go."

I stop in my tracks as chatty students flow past us. My heart is thumping like a galloping horse, and I really don't want to be alone with him.

"What?" He practically bites off my head with his blue eyes.

"Nothing. I, uh…let's just talk right here."

"What's wrong with my dorm room?"

"It's, uh…all the way over on the other side of campus."

"So is your dorm room. You think I'm going to do something to you, don't you? Some stupid prank."

I make a noncommittal shrug. "It's not outside the realm of possibilities."

"Fine. Let's go find a bench in the common." He heads for the exit, shaking his head, and I follow, trying not to notice the view. He's wearing soft faded jeans that hug his muscled ass like a glove.

My eyes dart to the safety of the back of his head. I don't want to drool over this guy, so I won't.

Before we get to the common, Hunter spots a bench underneath a maple tree between buildings. He goes to it, sits, and jerks his head for me to come on over. There's a hard look in his eyes, and his posture is rigid.

What the hell is up his ass? Now I can't help my curiosity.

I waltz over and take a seat. "Okay, what do you want to say?"

He doesn't speak, so I'm forced to sit there and stare, waiting for him. His handsome face is a little red and the muscle on his square, stubble-covered jaw is ticking away.

"Hunter, what's going on with you?"

He glances at me, but returns to looking out at nothing straight ahead.

"Okay." I can't stand feeling so uncomfortable, so I get to my feet.

"Wait." He grabs my arm, so I resume sitting and stare into those eyes.

"Well?"

"I, uhhh…I'll do it," he says.

"Do what?"

"Be your boyfriend. I'll help you get into the Tri-Kapps."

Oh, look. Somebody got himself another concussion.

I stand up. "Nice talking to you, but I'm not falling for your lame pranks." I turn to walk away, but before I know it, he's up and grabs my hand to slow me down.

He steps in front of me. "Yes. You are too smart to fall for pranks, which is why I'm proposing we strike a deal. We'll pretend to go out for a few weeks. I'll play your pussy-whipped boyfriend when we're around your friends, and I'll even let you break up with me in front of them."

"I don't understand." Why would he want to help me?

"I heard your roommate say that you had a bet going with them. I'm going to make sure you win."

"Why do you care if I win? What would you get out of it?"

"You know, uh…points. You'll come over to the party next weekend and make it clear you're willing to give it up. I get the points." He shrugs awkwardly. "It's a fair trade."

Tell the world I want to give my womanly flower to Hunter? A fair trade? Not even close. *Regardless…*

"You were way behind in the scavenger hunt, so I don't see how ten points will help."

He stares down at me for an awkward moment.

"What?" I ask.

"They, uh…increased the points," he mumbled.

"For what?"

"Sleeping with you. Sleeping with you is fifty points—it was Henry's idea."

"Oh, wow. That's not completely vile, sleazy, and immature. And such a shame that I'm not doing it, because you'd fit right in with that frat if you won." I step around him and continue walking, but he easily catches up and stands in my way again.

"We don't actually have to fuck, Tass. They just need to think we did."

"No. Absolutely not."

"Oh, I see, because I'm not good enough for

you." There's a bitterness in his voice that I just don't get.

"Uh, yeah. Exactly."

"Wow, you really can be a bitch sometimes," he snarls.

I shrug with a smile. "Takes one to know one. Bye, bitch." I turn to head in the other direction.

"Tassie, I can't afford the dorms anymore. If I don't get into the frat, I'll have to drop out."

I stop in my tracks. "Mothereffer." I sigh under my breath and then turn to face him with a growl. "That's not fair. You know full well that I am a complete sucker for people trying to get an education."

He flashes a coy, dimply smile that I'd rather not see right now, because—dammit—it's downright adorable and I know it's the look he uses to always charm the ladies.

"What happened to your scholarship money?" He received a full ride, according to the rumor mill.

"It paid for most of my tuition, books, and two hundred a month for room and board. But it's not enough and my parents can't afford to help. So that leaves me with the option of quitting football and getting a job, but quitting football means I'd lose the entire scholarship and I can't make enough to pay for everything."

"Oh." I'd heard a rumor that his dad's construction business wasn't doing well. I guess that rumor was true. I also knew, from my own experience, that

Hunter probably couldn't get much financial aid. His parents likely made just enough money to disqualify him. An academic scholarship was completely out of the question for him.

"Please, Tassie?"

I look at my pink low-top Converse, then at him, and back to the shoes. "Give me one good reason why I should help you?" Because I really, really need one. Especially since I feel like a complete moron for actually wanting to help him. It's like I can't resist rescuing the stray puppy who's bitten me a thousand times.

"We'd be helping each other," he explains. "I need a much cheaper place to live and you want to get into the Tri-Kapps."

"Ah!" I say, holding up my index finger. "But do I want it badly enough to let everyone think you've taken my pristine chariot out for its maiden voyage?"

"Your…chariot?"

"What would you like me to call it? My vaginal membrane? My cherry? My flower of purity? The winner's ribbon for my hump-day race?"

His handsome face contorts. "Chariot works."

"Great. And you're still not riding it."

"I didn't ask to. It's just something we'll let people think so I get the points. In exchange, for the next few weeks, I'll dote when we're around your uptight, intellectual elitist sorority sisters. And then you dump me. Simple."

I give it some thought—what it would mean to allow the blemish on my reputation.

"Come on, Tass. You know this is the best option for us both. Paweeeze?"

I look at Hunter, who has giant blue, anime-saucer eyes and a lower lip that's pouting for its life.

"No." I shake my finger at him. "Not the puppy face, Hunter."

He tugs on the hem of my T-shirt, his lower lip quivering. "Tassie…"

"Ugh. You are so juvenile. You know that, right?"

His face returns to its normal, annoyingly handsome perfection. "Yes. And thank you. You're making the right choice."

"Wait. I didn't agree to—"

He leans down and plants a big wet, closed-mouth kiss on my lips.

"Hey!" I step back.

"What?" He shrugs innocently. "You're my girlfriend now."

"No. I'm not and you need to—"

He grabs my hand tightly and starts pulling me along. "Come on, sugar rump. Let me walk you to your room."

"Hunter." I dig in hard with my heels and his hand slips from mine.

"Tassie."

"Hunter."

"Tassie…?" he warns with his voice as if to say,

"Don't be stupid."

I see that his plan has merit, but that doesn't make this any less ridiculous. Still, I would do almost anything to avoid the mental anguish associated with letting my family down and tarnishing the Summerset pride.

I give it a long, long moment of thought. None of this really matters as much as my long-term goals. And getting into that sorority, as horrible as this particular chapter is, will open doors the rest of my life. The sacrifice is worth it.

"Fine." I whoosh out a breath. "But there needs to be rules. Like…no kissing. And definitely don't call me sugar rump."

"No kissing?" He steps in close and places his large hands on his hips in such a way that pulls the fabric of his jeans tighter, making his bulge more pronounced.

The guy's packing. I suddenly feel moronic for calling him a shrimp dick. Clearly the world can see his member falls more into the category of a whale, if we are sticking to the whole sea-creature analogy. *He's more like Moby Dick, not shrimp dick.*

"Hey. Eyes up here, Tass."

Oh, jeez. I look up at him, pretending like that didn't just happen, but the glib expression on his face—one corner of his lips turned up and a proud twinkle in his eyes—hints that he enjoyed my checking him out.

He steps in a little closer and places his hands on my shoulders, speaking in that low, deep voice that sets off unwanted flutters in my stomach. "Tassie, how are we supposed to convince anyone that we're legit if we don't kiss?"

He's got me there, I think, unable to stop from checking out those soft lips. He's staring at mine, too, and starts to lean in a little.

I panic and stick out my hand. "Okay. Fine. But kissing is only allowed if I initiate."

"You want to be in control of the kissing?" He pffts.

"What? It frankly makes both our stories more credible. If your bros are watching, they'll see me throwing myself at you. If my sisters are watching, they'll see you waiting patiently for whatever I'm willing to give you since you will be my whipped man—a role you're clearly destined to play."

"Whipped," he scoffs. "That's never going to happen, but whatever. You can be in charge of kissing, even though we both know you don't know how."

"Yes, I do." I totally don't. In fact…I think I just had my first kiss.

Dammit! And it was Hunter? Oh, come on! No justice. There's no justice.

"Do you want me to show you?" he asks, in a low, quiet voice.

I think he's joking at first, but he's not smiling. He's dead serious.

Before I have a chance to think it through, I'm starting to open my mouth with the intention to say yes. I am curious to know what a real kiss might really feel like. But then I snap to my senses and realize who this is. Not my Prince Charming. Not the guy for me. He's my adversary.

"No, thanks," I say. "I think I'm good."

He holds out his large rough hand. "Hand-holding it is, then."

I hesitate but take it, which makes him grin. Genuinely grin.

Why's he enjoying this so much? He's supposed to hate me. *Maybe he likes making me feel uncomfortable,* which clearly this situation does.

"Stop that," I bark.

"What?" His grin spreads out like a contagious disease I want to cure.

"Don't act like this is some giant victory and I've forgotten all about our turbulent past."

His smug grin takes a dive and his brows knit together. "So you *do* remember?"

"Uh, hello. Who could forget you picking on them for thirteen years?"

"No. I meant the other thing."

"What other thing?"

He stares instead of answering. "Never mind. The past is the past for me. That's all that matters."

Okaaay. What's with him? "Whatever you say, Hunter."

His lips curl into a subtle smile that seems forced. "Come on. Let's get this over with." He takes my hand firmly in his and begins walking back to my dorm. "Sugar rump."

CHAPTER NINE

Hunter and I spent about an hour talking about "the plan" in my dorm room—yes, alone—not as bad as I thought, though I did find myself looking at his arms a lot. He would move them when he spoke, making them flex and bulge. They were so...so...muscly. Then Elle showed up and Hunter excused himself for some evening shenanigans at the Alpha House—no girls allowed. Some Cro-Magnon bonding idiocies to be sure.

After the requisite BSing with Elle, who absolutely knew I was up to something (but I was not about to drag her into my little plan), I updated my weekly planner.

Wednesday: Tri-Kapp Cap-Night. The Tri-Kapps would raise money, selling iced cappuccinos at the concession stand just outside the stadium during the big game against San Diego State, and Hunter and I would make our first public appearance. I would make it a point to go inside the stadium during the game and wave at him from the bleachers or catcall his name. He would make goo-

goo eyes at me before he disappeared into the lockers at halftime. I made it clear that I would not be initiating any kissing, but we could hug. He did not seem to care one way or another. About the not-kissing, I mean.

Fine by me. Because I don't want to have his wet, hot tongue inside my mouth. So good. We're on the same page.

Thursday night: Keg Run for Narcolepsy, hosted by the Alphas. *So appropriate.* After all, the Alphas spend most of their lives asleep and hungover.

Friday night: romantic movie-thon at the Tri-Kapp House. Hunter will so hate this, and I can't wait to make him sit through estrogen bombs like *Titanic* and *The Proposal* ("*Rrrramone!*"). On the other hand, I feel exceptionally nervous. Lainey and Jessica will be watching closely, and I'm unsure if Hunter can convince them that he's insanely into me simply because I used my big brain to break the code and turn him on with my hot body and lack of intellect. Because that is the other part of all this: Me demonstrating that my hypotheses were all true; I could get Hunter to want me simply by acting and dressing easy and stupid.

By the time Wednesday night finally rolls around, I've carefully run through the events in my mind and feel confident our little ruse will go off without a hitch. I've even had time to buy a few new outfits—a cute pair of red open-toed stacked heels, several extremely short skirts, and a few skimpy summer dresses that could be mistaken for nighties—and I got a light spray tan and mani-pedi with pearly pink polish. Honestly, I can't remember the last time I pampered myself or spent this much time on my appearance. So while these skimpy clothes might not be my usual fare, it kind of feels good to do something not directly related to academic advancement.

I stroll up to the rented barista cart just beside the walkway leading into the stadium, wearing my uniform for the evening—short blue skirt, sandals, and the mandatory Tri-Kapp Cap shirt, which I've sexied up by cutting out the neck so it hangs over one shoulder. Before I even check in with Lainey, I notice a pack of Gamma Nus going inside. They're all wearing pink T-shirts and holding little black pirate flags that say "The Treasure HUNT is On!"

Well, this ought to be interesting. Tonight, their "Hunt" will be doing the unthinkable: giving out a little nerd love to a Tri-Kapp. My team, however, has already been notified about the significant headway in my plot to prove brains beat brawn, and that by Friday, he'll be my Alpha bitch.

"Hi, Lainey," I say as she's taking an order and passing it over to the renta-caff guy.

"Tassie," she replies with a venomous grin. "So. I got your message. Tonight's the big night, huh? And love the outfit, by the way—Sluts-R-Us having a clearance sale so the trailer-park trash can afford some new hooker wear?"

She turns to Jessica, who's standing behind the counter, helping the barista guy, and raises her hands for a high ten.

"Good one, Lain!" Jessica snorts and dishes two palms.

I crinkle my nose at these two worthless snobs. "Well, the short skirt is obviously part of my little experiment—which is working successfully, I might add—however, the last time I checked, being poor and living in a trailer park doesn't make you a prostitute, trashy, or easy. It just makes you poor, and there's no shame in that. Nor is there shame in shopping clearance. Everyone loves to save money." I sigh and turn away to grab one of the signs leaning against the cart so I can get to work promoting our fundraiser. "There is, however, shame in being a stuck-up cunt," I mutter under my breath.

"Ex-cuse me!" Lainey barks.

Oops. I guess she heard me. With sign in hand, I pivot and smile. "What?"

Lainey comes out from behind the cart counter, bellies right up and sticks her nose in mine. "What did you just say to me?"

I laugh dismissively. "Uh, I said, 'Such a shame. Look how poorly these signs are cut.'" I hold mine up to demonstrate. "They're all crooked. See? Whoever did them didn't bother with the right angles. It's kind of annoying. Definitely not a good representation of the Tri-Kapps."

Lainey huffs. "You just watch yourself, Tassie."

"Okay." *Idiot.* I begin walking in the other direction, planning to stake out a spot over by Elle, closer to the parking lot and away from these two fascist princesses.

"Hey, Tassie!" Lainey barks. "We'd better see his full submission by Friday or you're going to the reject pile where you belong."

I look over my shoulder, and I'm about to throw out a smartass comment that will surely seal my fate, but then I spot Hunter strutting toward me. He's got on his skintight white pants, carrying his helmet, and showing off one hell of a smile—full-on dimples and everything. His bulge is an eyeful as well, not that I notice. Much.

With a smile, I watch him approach, but I'm also watching the expressions on Lainey's and Jessica's faces as he walks right by them as if they were completely invisible.

"Hey, what you doing out here?" I smile big and bright like I don't have a care in the world and I'm really happy to see him. Okay, I sort of am. I mean, only because he just stopped me from telling Lainey to stick it, of course. *No other reason*, I tell myself.

He walks right up and hugs me.

"Oh. Okay. We're doing this." I grunt as he squeezes the bejeezus out of me. "Okay, there, big man," I croak. "Go easy on the ribs."

"Mmmm…I missed you."

He tightens his grip, smashing my body against

his. He feels hard and hot. It's like being hugged by a marble statue that's been heated in the sun. I can't say I don't like it.

Wait. Oh, jeez. Is that his bulge? A tingle rockets down my spine. *And…lucky me. There's a reminder of my vitamin S deficiency.* Sex is a corporeal nutrient, right?

"Okay. That's really enough," I whisper. "You're poking me. With your *thing*, if you know what I mean."

"Oh, sugar rump. Don't be shy. It's just my little way of saying hi to a woman I find so attractive." He leans into me a little more.

"Hunter!" I hiss, trying to squirm away without being obvious.

I feel his body jiggling. The jackass is laughing. "It's just my athletic supporter," he whispers.

"Oh."

"But who knows what's underneath it? Could be just as firm," he says in that low, deep voice.

I scoff. "I don't want to know what you have going on down there."

He finally releases me and then beams down and pinches my chin. "Is this whipped enough for you," he turns up the volume so everyone can hear, "*sweetie pie?*"

I smile through my teeth. "Laying it on a little thick there, buddy."

"I just wanted you to know," he says loudly, "that I saved you a seat right in the front. I want my sugar rump right there watching the game."

I try not to crinkle my face, but I'm pretty sure I look like I've just swallowed a bee or cockroach.

"Gee. Thanks, *muffin nuts*," I growl loudly, with a smile.

"Muffin nuts?" he scowls.

"You can't help that they're all squishy from getting tackled all the time." I look to my side at some fans who are gawking as they pass and have clearly heard what I just said. "Like ripe avocados! Poor guy. I tell him to wear a cup, but—"

"Okay, Tassie. Point taken," he says. "So, see you during the game. Your seat is right next to Jennifer. Just look for the girl with the pink hat in the group of pink shirts."

Oh, great. He's got me sitting with the Gamma Nus.

"That's very thoughtful, Hunter."

He looks at his watch. "Oh, shit. I gotta go." He leans down and pecks me on the lips.

Dammit. He got me again! Now I'll never be able to lie to myself and claim that my first kiss technically didn't come from Hunter because I didn't kiss him back. I can't use that excuse twice. Seems like a stretch.

I continue holding on to my fake-as-hell smile. "Score a goal for me!"

He frowns and then jerks his head. "Uh…sure. Goal for you, babe." And then disappears inside the stadium.

I immediately realize I said goal, not touch-down, but he was nice enough not to sports-talk shame me. I glance over at Lainey and Jessica, who've witnessed the little show of man-whippedness.

They look like they've just observed a unicorn flying out of the sky or some other impossible crap. This time, I grin for real and then shrug at them.

They both glare and return behind the counter to fill orders.

Me? I'm happy as hell, and my body's all lit up with tingles and adrenaline. Clearly because Hunter came through for me.

The feeling melts away as I realize that I'm up next and have to act like I want to give it up to Mr. Football.

I'm not exactly sure how to do that.

Oh, I'll figure it out.

CHAPTER TEN

As soon as the game starts, the crowds around the concession area thin out, so I go inside to watch the game until halftime. I make my way to the pink section, where fifty-some odd Gammas are cheering and waving their Hunt-Pirates flags over something happening on the field. The rest of the Gammas are down in the action on cheerleading duty.

My eyes scan the front row of Pink Town, and I see a blonde girl in a pink hat. That must be Jennifer.

I make my way over, skootching by, careful not to spill beers or step on toes. "Hi, are you Jennifer?"

Her brown eyes look me over, mostly dragging over my shirt. "Oh, you're Hunter's little friend— the Tri-Kapp."

Little friend? "Uh, yeah. I'm Tassie."

"Well, take a seat!" She scoots over, creating a chain reaction of pink booties wiggling down the bench.

"Thank you." I'm immediately surprised by everyone's lack of snobbery.

"Any friend of Hunter's!" she yells over the cheering crowd. "That's Bea, by the way." She jerks her head toward the girl to my other side.

"Hi, nice to meet you," I say to Bea.

"Hey, Tri-tip! Welcome to the fun zone."

It takes a moment to noodle out that she's merely trying to be friendly with the "Tri-tip" comment. Bea immediately passes me a cold beer, and I reluctantly take the offering, not wanting to be rude. I don't drink. Or at least, I haven't drunk before, and I'm underage.

Well, I suppose one sip won't hurt. I don't want to be impolite.

I take a sip and want to spit out the bitter fuzzy liquid. Instead, I force myself to swallow it. "Mmmm...yummy."

Bea makes a little laugh. "Not a beer girl, huh?"

"Uh...no. It's great. Thank you." I take a gulp to show my appreciation.

Something happens on the field and everyone stands and begins booing. I look over, and Hunter is no longer visible.

"Oh, shit." He has to be underneath the huge pile of bodies in the center of the field. I stand, too, almost spilling my beer. "Is he okay?"

"We hope so," says Jennifer. "We're only five minutes into the game."

I can't breathe as I watch them peel the dogs off the dog pile, like layers of an onion.

Please be okay. Please be okay...

They remove the last guy, and there's Hunter lying facedown in the mud, a football gripped tightly in his hands. He then stands up with the aid of a few teammates, and the crowd goes wild. I have no clue what just happened other than my heart is pounding. My body is sweating. I think I just had my first panic attack.

I take another chug of beer to cool myself off.

Hunter looks my way for the briefest of moments, and I know he sees me, which is a bad thing. Because I'm not staying. I can't handle watching this—barbarianism. Violence and celebrating birthdays are phobias for me. I just don't like them. The violence because my mother and father are pacifists and drilled certain antiviolence ideas into my head. That time in the eleventh grade when I smacked Kurt Lipmann, for example? I don't even remember doing it. But I do remember feeling sick to my stomach and getting yelled at. So strange. As for my other phobia, birthdays, I simply don't like the idea of my body slowly degrading over the course of several decades. It's depressing. So I've got a strict rule about not celebrating my birthday, which is coming up in November. Not that I will give it any thought.

In any case, I can't stay and watch Hunter get hurt. I don't like it. But I also don't like the idea of letting him down. I haven't held up my end of the deal yet.

I start to think of options as the players on the

field do that whole setup thing where they face each other and bend over. I close my eyes. I can't watch.

The crowd is quiet and then everyone goes crazy, woohooing and screaming, "Go Pirates!"

Fuck. I have to look.

I open my eyes just as Hunter snaps the ball toward another guy all the way on the other side of the field.

There's no way the ball will get all the way there. It's impossible. But to my utter disbelief, that damned ball goes and goes and keeps on going until the guy on the other side snatches it from the air and then runs to the end.

Everyone yells, "Touchdown!"

"Oh, that's a touchdown, huh?" I mutter to myself, absentmindedly sipping my disgusting beverage that seems to be growing on me.

Our entire pink section stands up and starts chanting, "Hunt is on! Hunt is on!"

I have to admit I feel kind of good for him. I mean, these people, they love him. He's some sort of rock star in their minds. Still, I don't think I can stomach seeing him hurt again. And didn't they put out a movie about this sport, how it's really not good for the brain?

I can't believe I'm so worried about him.

Jennifer and Bea sit back down and the cheering dies.

"That was so freaking awesome, right?" says Jennifer.

"Sure. Awesome," I say.

"So how did you know Hunter?" she asks.

"Oh, uh." I'm not sure what he's told them, so I say something obvious. "He hates math, so I agreed to help him."

"Do you have a class together?"

"Uh, no. I'm taking Modeling and Differential Equations for the Life Sciences."

"Oh. I won't take that until my sophomore year, but I'm looking forward to it."

Have I entered a black hole and merged with an alternate universe once again? "Seriously? What's your major?"

"Economics. I don't technically need that class, so it'll be an elective."

"Ohmygod. Me too. I'm a bioengineering major, but I think I might do a double degree depending on how things go."

"Bea's a double major. Marketing and Economics."

"Really?" I look at Bea, who shrugs.

"Couldn't make up my mind." Bea looks back at the field. "Go Pirates!"

I'm thoroughly shocked that these two Gamma Nus are so academically focused and nothing like their reputation. They're also pretty friendly, which is more than I can say for my sisterhood.

"So you're tutoring The Hunt, huh? What's that like?" asks Jennifer, casually watching the players get set for the next…thingy.

I really want to leave before I am subjected to watching these cement trucks in helmets park on top of Hunter again.

"I'm not exactly tutoring him," I say, "but I am intending to sleep with him. Very soon. My first time, you know."

Jennifer freezes and then starts busting up. Bea too.

Jennifer smacks my knee so hard that beer splashes down my leg. "You're funny, Tri-tip!"

Her laughter dies down when she realizes I'm not laughing with her. To be honest, I'm not quite sure what's so funny, anyway.

"Wait. You're serious?" she says.

"Yeah. Why not?" I shrug. "I mean, I'm a red-blooded American girl. He's a horny guy. And who better to crack open the dam of promiscuity than the Huntsman, The Hunt, Mr. Bigdick himself?" I smile politely and bat my eyelashes, hoping she'll buy my obscenities and then spread the news. Yes, for the record, I am absolutely dying of embarrassment on the inside.

"Well, sweetie, good luck with that." She turns to watch the game.

I don't want to feel insulted, but I do. "Why? You think I'm not pretty enough?"

"What?" she scoffs. "No. You're totally adorable with your whole," she waves her hand over my body, "sexy hipster look."

Sexy hipster? I'd been going for just good old-fashioned slut, but hey. Sexy hipster sounds kind of cool.

She continues, "Anyway, I'm sure any guy here would jump you, but Hunt there is untouchable."

Huh? "What do you mean untouchable? Does he have an STD?"

She laughs. "I wouldn't know. But he's got someone back home. He won't even look at another girl. And trust me, we've all tried."

"Back at home? Who?" I ask.

"Hell if I know, but she's one lucky girl."

Okay, this has to be a lie. A complete lie. Because if he had a steady girlfriend back home, I'd know. Wouldn't I?

My mind shuffles back to Elle's comment regarding Hunter being in love. Then my brain starts throwing out all the facts to shoot down that theory. He's about as faithful as a honeybee. The more flowers, the better.

Jennifer hands me a flag. "Here. You'll need this."

I take it and stare at the thing. "Why?"

"It's as close as any of us are ever gonna get to action with Hunter."

Suddenly, Elle's other comment flashes in my mind. *I think he was into you. Big time.*

Shut the front door. I know her comments are ridiculous and unfounded—she doesn't know jack. Or jill. But the fucking kicker is that my heart goes into cardiac-lite, thumping out of control at the thought of him wanting me.

I shoot from my seat, like I'm about to declare independence in a room full of oppressive aristocrats. *I say there, old boy! You are out of order. We are free men. And free men we shall stay!*

"Tassie? You okay?" asks Jennifer.

I nod stiffly and try to choke down a nonexistent crumb in my throat. "Sure. Super good. I have to…to…" I point toward the concession area. "Get ready for halftime cappuccinos."

Bea raises a brow. "You have at least another fifteen minutes until halftime."

"Yeah, but…"

Jessica places her hand on my arm. "Stay, Tassie. I know you Tri-Kappas hate us, but we're really not so bad."

The sincerity in her eyes makes me feel horrible. I don't want her to think I'm a hater. Because I'm not. *Am I?*

I sit down. "I actually think Greek rivalry is pretty stupid."

Jessica wraps an arm around me and squeezes. "You're pretty smart for a Tri-tip, Tassie."

I finally manage to swallow that lump in my throat. "Thanks." This is the first time in my life that I've ever felt so welcomed. Ever. And it kind of makes me want to cry. Here I'd hated them for judging me, only to discover I was the hater, assuming all sorts of things.

Maybe I'm not as smart as I thought. At the

very least, I'm lacking education. Education about people.

This is a startling awakening. But the evidence is sitting right beside me. Two perfectly nice people I had no business judging or disliking.

I have to wonder what else I'm under-informed about.

I raise my plastic cup to Jessica and then Bea. "Go Pirates."

They smile in a way that makes me feel like they see me. They don't judge. And more importantly, they're real women with goals who know how to have fun.

And like me, they don't have Hunter. Not that I want him. Just stating the obvious.

CHAPTER ELEVEN

"You really should come with me, Elle. The Gammas are nice. I mean, really nice," I say, pulling a short little summer dress with yellow and white flowers over my head.

"Thanks, but I'm just not a big beer drinker. And we have a bio quiz tomorrow."

"Thus the reason I'm not drinking and only going for an hour." Really, just long enough to put on a show for Hunter's frat buddies. They all need to know I'm planning to let him mount the white pony, slay the V-dragon, crack the seal.

Why do I keep coming up with this weird virginal slang? I suppose it helps make the topic more comfortable. In any case, once I show everyone that the big virgin is ready and willing to throw in the white towel—*Crap, I did it again!*—lose her virginity to Hunter, the rest will be up to him. He has to tell everyone that he slept with me.

I quickly start thinking about the "girl back home" Jennifer mentioned. This can't be right. I'll have to talk to him.

"Sure you don't want to come for a little while?" I say to Elle. "We can laugh at the meatheads? Say big words and watch them get confused?" I joke.

From her desk, which is pushed against the foot of her bed like mine, she sighs with frustration. "Sounds entertaining, but I'm not in the mood."

I suddenly realize that staying behind to study isn't the real reason she won't go.

"Is everything okay?" I ask.

"Sure." She looks down at her notebook.

"Sure, as in 'yes'? Or sure, as in 'I don't want to talk about it'?"

"Both."

I don't like that answer.

I sit down on her bed so I can see her face. "What happened?"

"I don't want to talk about it, remember?"

It's got to be her mother. Something not good. "Okay, but I'm here if you want to talk."

She nods but doesn't reply. I want to help her. I want to say something that will make her feel better and know that she'll get through this. But what do I know? My mother isn't the one dying. Still, the thought of what Elle is going through makes me want to cry. Just full-on bawl right here. It's just too sad.

No. That won't help her. She needs sympathy, not empathy. That's what my mother said once when I asked her how she dealt with people dying in their trials. First, she explained that it's part of the work—keep testing, keep reformulating, keep going until someday they stop dying. "That's all that matters, Tass. We can't give up." Still, I knew from the look in her eyes that it pained her not to be able to save people yet. Her failure meant their deaths, which would be a heavy burden on anyone. Perhaps it's the reason I want to follow in her footsteps. I don't want her to have to suffer through this alone. And I don't want her to ever give up, so I want to be there to help.

As for sympathy versus empathy, that was the second thing she told me about. Sympathy is filled with compassion, but keeps you strong so you can lift others when they're down. You keep your head on straight, but you still care.

Empathy is dangerous.

Their despair becomes your own, and you feel as though it's happening to you. You're of no use to anyone once you cross that line. Because someone needs to be there at the top of the mud pit, holding the rope, telling them to grab it and climb out. You can't do that if you jump inside with them.

Regardless, I can't help feeling my feet slide down that muddy embankment. Just a little. What Elle is going through, watching someone she loves die, is my worst nightmare.

I blink away the threat of tears and take hold of the rope.

"Nope. Nope. I'm not taking no for an answer." I stand up. "You're taking a one-hour mental vacation from your life." I grab her hand and start pulling. "You need it. And it's only four o'clock. You'll have plenty of time to come back and study."

She stays seated. "I'm really not in the mood."

I look down at her big brown eyes and messy blonde hair, trying to find the right words to get through to her. *It's okay to live and smile a little, even though she's dying; otherwise you can't stay strong for her,* I want to say, but those words are too harsh.

"I know," I say quietly so she understands that *I* understand.

She draws a deep breath. "Fine. One hour."

"Yay!" I let go of her hand and clap. "I promise, at the very least, it will be entertaining."

"What is this event again?"

"Keg run for narcolepsy. Or something like that."

She shakes her head. "Oh boy. Sounds enlightening."

"Only if you check your IQ at the door."

She chuckles. "Didn't plan on bringing it anyway."

There is no door to check our IQs at, we discover, as Elle and I arrive to the Alpha House and are immediately redirected by the signs to go to a park a few blocks over. Despite the sun setting, the September heat is sweltering today, and I'm praying they're serving ice-cold water.

"So what exactly is a keg run?" asks Elle as we follow the crowd toward an area of the park that's been blocked off with rope. Alphas in white T-shirts that say "Security" are stationed around the perimeter for the purpose, I assume, of keeping people from sneaking in.

My eyes scan the crowd inside and around the cordoned-off area, searching for Hunter. I don't see him.

"Not sure," I reply to Elle. "I'm guessing they're selling beer for charity. Like we sold cappuccinos."

We come up to a long line of people waiting to get inside the party area, and I quickly realize we're not getting in. "Twenty-one and over."

She steps to the side and takes a look at the sign for herself. "Well, let's go back. I'm not paying five dollars to go over a rope and watch people drink beer, anyway."

I can't argue with that, but I'm here for another reason, too. And there he is.

"Ah, but look." I point to a crowd over on the other side of the field. "We don't have to pay to watch the entertainment."

We both see Hunter and about ten other guys in their football jerseys, shoulder pads, and shorts, getting ready to lift what I can only assume are full kegs.

"Heeeey, Tassie," says a deep voice to my side.

I look up to see a giant tree trunk. "Henry,

how's it going?"

"Fine," he wiggles his brows, "now that you're here, baby."

Baby? Oh, wait. "Sorry, buddy. Don't waste your time. I'm not giving up the V-card to you." *Dang, I did it again. Why can't I sound like an adult when I talk about sex?*

Henry's face contorts into something resembling confusion.

"Yes, Henry," I say, "I know about the scavenger hunt, which is why I've decided that Hunter's getting the points."

"What are you talking about?" Elle looks at me.

I look at Elle and contemplate if I should tell her the truth. I didn't want to make her an accomplice, but she'll probably figure out our sham. It was her idea in the first place.

I smile at her. "Yeah, sleeping with me is supposedly worth fifty points now. It was Henry's idea, actually."

Henry looks busted—big green eyes, mouth falling open, red face. "Well, I only—"

"That's horrible!" Elle barks at him. "Who would do such a thing? Do you have a sister?" She places her fists on her hips and glares at him.

"Well," he scratches the back of his head, "yeah. I have three."

"How would you feel if some guys made getting into their pants a stupid game?"

"I'd be mad," he says dejectedly.

It is completely barbaric, and I love that Elle just made Henry see the light.

"Sorry, Tassie," Henry says in a quiet voice. "We were kinda drunk when we came up with that. I'll talk to the guys and have them take it down."

What? No. If they do that, then Hunter will lose the points. "No need. Just promise you'll never put sex on the board again. But us women will let it slide. Just this once."

"But, Tassie," Elle cuts in, "that's just—"

I give her a wink-wink to convey hush-hush. "I've already decided that Hunter gets to nail the virgin. It's going to be awesome." I sound like an imbecile.

Elle crinkles her nose. "Okaaay."

"It's starting. I gotta go," says Henry. "Did you place your bets?"

"Bets?" Elle asks.

"Yeah, pick your winner over there." Henry points to another table not too far from the beer corral's entrance. "If your horse wins, your name goes into the drawing for a date."

"With who?" I ask.

"The winning horse."

I see out of the corner of my eye that the guys on the other side of the field are lifting the kegs and placing them on their shoulders.

"You mean you guys are going to race, carrying kegs?"

"Yeah, man. It's a keg run. You really need to

stop smokin' so much weed." Henry turns away and heads for the pack of "horses."

I shrug at Elle and make a little loop with my finger over my temple to indicate Henry is crazy. She nods, knowing I'm not a pothead. *Ah, but the day is still young...*

Meanwhile, I realize Elle keeps glancing toward the direction we came from. She wants to leave.

"Come on. I'll buy you a ticket," I say.

"No. This is silly."

"Of course. But it's for charity, and I'm sure narcolepsy is one of those overlooked disorders, since the people are always too sleepy to drive awareness for their cause."

"You're such a smartass, Tassie."

"It's a gift."

We walk over, and I buy her a ticket for Henry. I get a ticket for Hunter. Apparently, the "horses" have to lap the park three times, hauling a full keg. Sounds brutal, to be honest.

The gun goes off just as we step away from the ticket table. Right away, I can see Hunter is not going to win this. The other guys, like Henry, look like rhinos carrying rolls of toilet paper on their shoulders. One guy is actually running with the barrel pressed into his chest like he's carrying a baby. Hunter is a big strong guy, but more like a chee-tah—lean and muscular—not a bulldozer built for hauling boulders.

Still, I can't help smiling because *he's* laughing

his ass off, struggling to keep his keg balanced.

"Oh! Come on, Hunter! Run!" I yell.

He sees me and shakes his head. The pack of rhinos are leaving him in the dust.

"Go, Henry!" screams Elle, to my side.

"You realize you're probably the only one who has a ticket for Henry, right?" I ask.

She blinks and realizes that if he wins, she'll likely be picked to go on a date with him.

"Go, Hunter!" she screams with a smile. "Go, anyone but Henry!" Luckily, Henry can't hear her over all the yelling.

"Hey, Tassie!" says a cheery voice to my side.

I turn and see Jennifer in a Got Sleep? T-shirt.

"Hi. Nice to see you again," I say.

She gives me a big hug that takes me by surprise.

"Uh, this is my roomie, Elle," I say after Jennifer releases me.

"Nice to meet you." Elle flashes her gapped teeth. It's kind of cute the way she smiles. Reminds me of a little bunny rabbit or something.

"Same here," Jennifer bounces up and down. "Who'd you guys get tickets for?"

"Henry." I point to Elle and then raise my hand. "Hunter for me."

"Awww…so sweet," Jennifer says enthusiastically. "Never give up hope." She holds out her fist, and I realize it's that fist-bump thing. That's definitely not proper geek etiquette, but I reciprocate anyway and do the whole hand explosion thing like I've seen in movies.

The pack of muscle heads shuffle by, grunting and sweating, and I go back to cheering for Hunter. He's literally laughing so hard, he's about to fall over as he passes us. I realize he's holding his keg all wrong with the curve of the barrel pressed into his neck. With his shoulder width and body mass, the weight of the keg is resting more on the outside of his shoulder.

"How much do you think that weighs?" I ask Elle.

"My guess? It holds about fifteen to eighteen gallons of liquid and water weighs approximately eight point three five pounds per gallon. So with the metal container included, I'd say the keg weighs one sixty to one seventy." She shrugs. "Just a guess."

"That's a fair guess." I ballparked one fifty, but she's smarter than me, so I go with her number. And Hunter is about six two and probably weighs about two twenty.

I break from the crowd and run to his side. "Switch to the flat side! Put the bottom of the keg on your shoulder and tip it inward toward you."

Panting, he gives me a look. "Huh?"

"Shift more of the weight toward your center, bonehead."

He rolls his eyes and winces, but then stops, wrestles with the one sixty (or eighty) pound beast and maneuvers it up on to his shoulder pad. He slides his hand through the slot at the top, which he barely reaches.

"Better?" I ask.

"Better. Thanks, my little nerd."

I frown, and he winks.

"Get off the track!" the crowd starts yelling at me.

"Okay." I hold up my hands and go back to the spectator position.

Before we know it, Hunter is closing the gap.

"Ha! There, you see. Math isn't a waste of time!" I yell at Hunter as he approaches us on the second lap, looking like he's going to keel over but still managing to hold his position in the middle of the pack of Incredible Hulks.

"I don't need math. I have my nerd princess," he barks back.

I laugh and watch him move toward the front. His arms are straining, biceps rippling, neck muscles pulsing and legs charging.

He looks pretty sexy. Not that I care.

Soon, they're on the third lap, approaching the finish line near us, when the crowd of a few hundred people amp up the cheering and the horses' egos kick in.

"Go, Hunter! Move that tight ass!" I yell.

Elle gives me a look.

"What? It's really tight," I say.

She shakes her head, but laughs anyway.

Hunter is almost to the end, second place, behind Henry of all people. Suddenly, I see Hunter step on something, twist his ankle, and the keg goes flying. He follows.

"Oohhh…" The crowd winces in unison.

I cover my mouth. "Oh no." I hope he's not hurt. Of course, none of the contestants stop to help him because they're all genetically part caveman and must win the race.

I run along the side of the track and go to him.

Hunter's clutching his ankle, rolling on his back, groaning.

"Oh shit. Are you okay?" I ask.

"Yeah, just…ahhh…give me a minute."

Elle comes up. "Is he all right?"

"It looks like he sprained it or something."

"I'll go get ice." She scurries off, and I kneel beside him with my hands sort of doing this weird tapping thing on his arm. I don't know if I'm supposed to touch him or not touch him or what to do. I realize I know almost nothing about sports injuries, but I can do the Heimlich and CPR.

Henry and a couple of the guys, all out of breath and dripping with sweat, finally come over.

"Dude, you okay?" Henry says.

"I think I sprained it." Hunter groans.

"No. Fuck no, dude. We have a game on Saturday," says one of the guys, who I really want to kick.

"He's in pain, you moron," I say. "Help him up so we can get him over to one of those tables."

Henry reaches down and scoops up Hunter as if

he were a little rag doll.

"My fucking hero," Hunter grunts.

"Shut up. I'm trying to help, bro," Henry grunts.

They march past Elle, who's already holding a bag of ice.

"That's kind of adorable, isn't it?" she says to me.

"Errr…sure."

Sadly, I'm now being shallow, too, because I'm already thinking about our plan and whether or not this will interfere.

Nothing wrong with making sure the show goes on.

I follow Henry inside the beer playground as they sit Hunter down in a fold-out chair and prop his leg up on another. Elle's quickly got the bag of ice in place.

"I hope it's just a light sprain because I'm really looking forward to having sex tonight like you promised," I say loudly.

Everyone around us falls into a dead hush and stares at me, including Hunter, whose blue eyes are shooting WTF arrows.

"Sorry," I mouth. "Too much?"

"Uh, yeah," he snarls under his breath.

"Ha. Ha. Hahaha…" I laugh exaggeratedly loud. "Just messin' around."

The festivities continue, and I kneel beside him.

"What was that?" he growls.

"I'm sorry, okay. I just didn't want to let everything get derailed because you decided to participate in the Thor-a-thon for beer lovers."

"Harrumph!" He looks away and jerks his head at a few Gammas standing in their tiny tees and short-shorts, looking over and chatting about him.

"Hey, eyes over here, buddy." I point to my face.

"What? They're just friends."

"No, genius," I hiss, "they're not. Because nobody is going to believe we slept together if you're not at least pretending to be into me and, by the way, when were you going to tell me about the girl back home?"

Hunter's chiseled features—cheekbones, perfect brows, straight nose and jaw—look like they've been washed away in a flash flood.

"I don't know what you're talking about."

My brows furrow. "Bullcrap."

"It is bullcrap. I have no idea what you're talking about."

"Oh, really?" I stand up and cross my arms. "Then let's ask some of the girls here what they know—" I turn.

"Wait. Fine." He leans in from his chair. "It's just a story I made up—you know. To keep them away."

"Why?"

The color returns to his face, but his expression is as serious as...okay, yes, a damned heart attack. I'm saying it again, okay?

"I can't afford to fuck this up, Tassie," he whispers.

"What?"

"This," he hisses. "It's my only chance."

My mind usually outsmarts me, meaning it sees patterns and relationships before I ask it to. Images and thoughts, facts and memories flood my mind. Hunter's big change the summer before last, his father's business going under, the fights I've overheard for years flowing out of their garage—so many strong, harsh words coming from his dad that I often wondered how he could manage a smile the next day. Stupid. Loser. Lazy. The kinds of words that would scar me for life if my father or mother ever said them aloud. I know this because my own parents have merely implied they think these things about me and I ended up in the fetal position. Conclusion being that if I were him, I'd want to get away, too.

"What happened that summer before senior year?" I ask.

He jerks his head back, and toxic fury sparks in his intense blue eyes. His nostrils flare and the veins in his neck visibly throb. The rage is so palpable that I step back without even knowing it. I've pissed him off. I've hurt him. And I don't know why. I only know that while I should show this guy no mercy after all the pain he's caused me, mercy is the only thing I want to give.

"I-I'll go," I say.

"Yeah, good choice," he scowls, still seated.

"O-okay." I bob my head. "I hope your ankle's okay."

He replies with a turn of the head, and my heart sinks into the mud. I can't breathe. Not that I really want to. It's like that pain inside him is in me.

Toxic empathy. Why? Why the fuck would I care and have such strong emotion for this gorgeous asshole? He's had everything handed to him for as long as I can remember, and I've succeeded despite him. Still, my thoughts don't match my heart, which knows I'm missing something.

I can't do this, I think. I can't operate in this space where I don't know the rules or facts or understand the variables. I just feel bad. Really fucking bad.

Before I know it, I'm just standing there looking down at him, blinking back fat tears. I don't know where they came from, just like I don't know why I'm so upset or emotional or biting my lower lip so goddamned hard that I taste copper. I'm a cold mess inside.

I need to go. Without another word, I turn and leave. There's this noise in my head, voices and conversations from the past that I don't remember ever seeing or hearing until now.

I don't stop until I've reached my dorm room, where I slam the door, climb into my bed, and pull the covers over my head.

What is happening to me? What *the fuck* is happening to me?

CHAPTER TWELVE

Friday morning, I'm up and showered before Elle. I head to my English class and push away the disturbing thoughts that haunted me the night before. I know whatever's jabbing at the back of my mind, it's not small. I know it's horrible, life-changingly bad.

By one o'clock, I'm fairly sure that whatever this is, it's going to trouble me until I confront it. But that's the thing. I don't know what it is. I only know two things: I don't want to remember it. And, two, neither does Hunter because he's never mentioned it—whatever "it" is.

I skip history and biochem and head straight to Hunter's dorm. Ten minutes of knocking on his door tells me he's not there. Standing in the hall, two floors above mine, I'm about to head for the Alpha House, but think twice. Even if Hunter's not playing today, he'll be at practice.

I turn and head for the stairs. I don't remember walking to the stadium. I don't remember climbing the stairs to the bleachers or looking down on the field. I only know Hunter is shaking me, saying my name. "Tass. Tass?"

I blink and gaze into his eyes. "Hunter?"

"Tass, what's going on?" he asks.

I'm a wreck, that's what. I must look like a crazy person because he looks worried. Really worried.

"I don't know," I say, looking down at my feet. "What happened, Hunter?" I look up at him, and it all explodes. My memories: Blood. Screaming. Staring into Hunter's eyes as he's asking why I won't say anything, why I'm pretending like I don't remember. I'm telling him he's stupid and crazy, that I don't know what he's talking about, which only upsets him more.

But now I do remember.

"Fuck." I cover my mouth. "Did you kill someone?" I whisper.

Because all I see is a memory of Hunter doing just that. And I think it's because of me.

"Drink this," Hunter shoves a bottle of water into my hands. I have only a vague recollection of going to his room, but I know it's his. His framed high school jersey hangs on the wall.

He lifts the bottle to my lips. "Drink."

I sip, but I'm not thirsty. I'm sad. I'm confused.

"What's going on, Hunter?" I whisper.

"Payback," he mutters and hobbles over, sitting

down on the bed beside me. His ankle is bandaged and he has ice packs strapped to it. He folds his large hands in his lap. "You really don't remember?"

"No," I whisper. "Not everything."

"They hurt you. I stopped them. That's about the gist of it."

I wince and look at his face, searching for some hint of what the hell he's talking about. "Who? When?"

He looks away.

"Hunter? Fucking tell me."

He wrings his hands so hard that *I* physically feel the pain. "It was the last weekend in July. I just got home from football camp."

I blink and suck in a sharp breath. None of this sounds remotely familiar, but there's a pain in my chest I'm too smart to ignore.

"What. Happened?" I prod.

He shrugs. "We were drunk. You were walking home."

"And?"

"At first they just pulled over and said some stuff to you. I didn't even realize who they were talking to. But then I heard your voice—you were yelling at them, telling them off or something. They got pissed and got out of the car. They wanted to throw you in. They...wanted to do things to you."

I press my hands over my heart. "What the fuck? And *you* let them?" *Why don't I remember? Why?*

His head whips up. "No. I didn't."

My neck muscles contract. My stomach knots. My hands fist.

"That's the fucking problem," he says. "I *didn't* let them."

As expected, my mind offers explanations I don't ask for. But in the recesses of my memories, I see Hunter pushing one guy back and then a fist hitting Hunter in the jaw. Then I see Hunter's hands hit back. I think I know this guy fighting with him. He's older than us by a few grades. Some jock Hunter used to hang out with when he was a freshman or sophomore—I'm not sure.

I see more flashes—like snapshots in a photo album—of the other guys pulling Hunter off the body on the ground he's beating to a pulp. Hunter stands and stares down at the immobile lump on the ground. It's dark, but the headlights of the car, facing away, are enough for me to see there's blood. A lot of blood. Hunter looks at me and says, "Run, Tassie. Run home. You were never here."

Trembling, I take a sip from the water bottle in my hand, my heart racing. I just can't understand where these memories went or why Hunter never said anything.

I let out a slow breath. "All this time, I figured it was your dad or girl problems."

Hunter gets up and sits across from me on his roommate's bed. "No."

"Did you kill him?" I ask in a quiet voice, because I don't really want to know, but I must.

"Almost."

"Thank God." In my memory, the guy looked dead. "How come I never heard anything about this?"

"I was a minor. The other guys weren't. I told them if they didn't say I acted in self-defense, I would make sure everyone knew what they really were up to that night—why I stepped in. So they agreed. And they agreed to keep you out of it so they wouldn't go through life with a sexual-predator tag on their names."

"But still, I think I would've heard something in the news or…" I run my hands through my hair.

"My parents agreed to settle with the other guy's family out of court if they kept it out of the press, but there were days and weeks and months when I wasn't sure what would happen. I kept expecting the police to show up and arrest me, and then there was you and trying to keep you out of all that. It was a fucking nightmare."

Oh fuck. Oh fuck. I stand, cross over to him and sit beside him. My heart is pounding so fast, and I want to throw up. I'm in shock.

"Thank you," I whisper, facing forward. I don't know what else to say. I used to think I was strong, I was smart, but now I'm just human. Weak, flawed, vulnerable. I spent all this time caring about something that wasn't real—Hunter was just some stupid jock and I was better than him. My destiny and self-worth were hinged upon becoming a Tri-Kapp. I didn't do better in school because I was picked on. These were just a few of the lies I'd been telling myself.

None of it was true or important or real.

This is real. And I'm wholly unequipped to deal with any of it.

"Thank you," I repeat.

CHAPTER THIRTEEN

Later that afternoon, I wake to a set of warm arms wrapped around my body. The bliss of being snuggled next to a strong man is quickly overridden by two things: one, I'm not quite sure where I am at first, and when I remember, the memory of this morning's conversation is included.

Oh, God. This is really happening.

I don't know how I feel, other than I'm grateful and sad. Hunter nearly ended someone's life two summers ago, and it was because he'd cared enough to step in. The rest, I assumed, was a question of legal acrobatics to keep him out of hot water. But the financial burden on his family…

Oh God. This is why his parents can't afford to help out with school. It's because of me and all the money they had to pay to keep it quiet.

I slide my cheek over Hunter's chest, feeling the heat of his body against mine and the soft murmur of his heartbeat in my ears. Now that I'm awake, really awake, I can't sort out our next steps.

Are there any?

Everything I've just now learned is in the past. Done. And talking more about this seems unnecessarily painful. Especially for him, and I don't want that. I don't want him to suffer any more than he has. But still, I need to talk about this or process or something, and talking to anyone else is betrayal. That leaves me with one option: pretending.

It never happened. We move on. He goes in his direction, and I go in mine. But that's not what I want either.

"Tass, you awake?" Hunter says, rubbing my arm with his callused hand.

"Yeah. I guess I didn't sleep much last night and it got to me." Really, I think my brain needed to shut down for a few hours, because my heart is in pain. How could I not know all this?

"You okay?" he asks.

"I'm not sure, but…" I sit up and rub my face. I need to be smart and handle this the right way. For him. Not for me. "I want to say something."

"Okay."

"I want…" I hesitate for a moment, reaching for the right words. "First, you need to know that there are no words to express how grateful I am."

"Okay."

"And I can only imagine what you went through and how hard you've had to work to put this behind you."

"Okay."

I continue, "So you should know that just because we never speak again doesn't mean that I won't be thinking of this every day for the rest of my life."

He sits up, blinking those blue eyes at me. "Did you just say you're never speaking to me again?"

I hold out my hand. "Wait. That didn't come out right. What I meant is that I can see I'm just a reminder of this—this horrible thing that happened, and I feel like you deserve better. You deserve to put it behind you."

"Tass, I have."

"Have you? Because the look on your face when you told me and the—"

"I'm fine."

"But how can you even stand to look at me?"

"For such a smart person, you can be a little dense sometimes, Tass. *You* didn't do anything. Those assholes did. So I did something back because there was no way I would've let them hurt you. Not ever."

"Oh." His words shock me a little and leave me wanting to ask why. But that would sound ungrateful and bitchy, like I don't think of him as a good guy capable of doing heroic things. Clearly, that's just not true. He's maybe the bravest person I've ever met.

Unlike me. I buried it all like a complete coward.

"So…I'm not just some horrible reminder of the night your life went to hell?" I ask.

He smiles and shrugs. "Well, maybe just a little.

But you'd irritate me either way, so I don't see the difference." His little smile turns into a shit-eating grin.

"Ha-ha."

"And it resulted in having to take some anger-management classes, which I can't say were all bad. It's definitely helped me mature. Unlike you."

He gives me a little push, and I nearly fall off the bed, but he catches my arm and pulls me closer.

"Hey," I protest but suddenly realize our noses are inches from each other and our eyes are locked. That feeling in my stomach hits me hard—uneasy flutters and knots and—

"Wow." I jolt to my feet. "I should go." I point over my shoulder. "I have stuff to do, like…" *Quick. Say something nerdy and convincing.* "Like alphabetize my underwear."

"Sure." He looks a little—okay, I don't know—amused, I suppose.

"We'll talk soon." I start backing toward the door.

"What about tonight?"

"Tonight?" I ask.

"The chick-flick thing at the Tri-Kapp House."

"Oh. I completely forgot about that." I suddenly feel like none of that matters. "I think," I crinkle my nose, "it's time for me to reevaluate that whole thing."

"I thought you really wanted to get in to that sorority."

"I don't know what I want." Everything feels different for me because this isn't a game anymore.

This is real. Very real. And so are my feelings, which are a mess because they're telling me that Hunter means a lot more to me than I realized and perhaps he always did. More shockingly, I might mean a lot more to him, too. Or not. *It's a lot to process. A lot.*

"You want to quit?" he asks.

Why did he have to use that word? Quitting is practically losing, and that's my Achilles' heel.

"No. I'm not saying that."

"You want me to still tell everyone we slept together?"

I don't even know what to say. I mean, I suppose a deal's a deal, but I wonder if we shouldn't throw in the towel. *Okay, but he just told you he saved you from those guys. Let him get his points so his housing situation is resolved.*

"Was it any good?" I ask.

He flashes one of those dimpled smiles. "The best."

"I don't know, Hunt. I think it was a little, fast. I mean, I can't even remember it, so…"

His jaw drops. "It was good. Amazing. You had the time of your life and orgasmed three times."

Hunter simply saying those words instantly sets me off. My nipples tighten, my core tingles, and I need to get the hell out of here.

"Okay. Sure. Yep. Three screaming Os! See ya!"

I jerk open the door.

"Where are you going?"

Clearly, I'm a coward and running away from you because I'm not ready to feel like I already do. Dammit! I'm not making any sense again, I think as I'm speed walking down the hall.

"Hey," Hunter screams, "you forgot your panties, so I'll bring them by at seven when I pick you up for movie night!"

Horrified, because the handful of students lurking in the hallway are staring and smiling, I glance over my shoulder.

Nice, Hunter. Real nice. Of course, my panties are right where I left them—on my ass—so he's just doing it to mess with me. Case in point, he's desperately trying not to crack up.

I'm about to throw out some vengeful comment about tiny penises, but I realize I don't feel much like playing the hate game anymore. Just like I'm not quite sure I want to continue the charade—at least for myself—or get into the Tri-Kapps. I really want to step back and reevaluate the whole enchilada. Including these feelings I have for Hunt.

Oh, God. I think I'm in love with him. And perhaps I have been for years.

I take the stairs, absolutely desperate for a big fat smart brain to converse with so I can process. I won't tell Elle about what Hunter did to those guys—not my secret to tell—but I will explain the crux of it. She'll get the picture. She'll know what to do.

I get to my room, slip my key from my pocket, and open the door. "Hey, Elle! I—" I immediately realize she's not alone. In fact, I'm staring at a huge pair of shoulders and a bare muscled ass wedged between two small kneecaps.

"Holy shit!" I close my eyes. "Oh, God. I'm so sorry," I turn, slam the door shut behind me, and stand in the hallway.

I can't believe it. Little Elle was getting down and dirty!

The door opens and out steps Henry in his boxers, his clothes and shoes all wadded up in front of his crotch. "Hey, Tass. Wassup." He jerks his head and strolls away nonchalantly.

I can't believe this. I just…can't.

I go inside my room and see Elle in her bathrobe with her freshly fucked hair.

"Hey, Tass," she says casually.

"Don't hey Tass me. You screwed Henry?"

She shrugged. "I prefer the words *had sex* or *intercourse*, but yeah, we humped like a couple of randy farm animals."

Okay then. "And how did this come about?"

"I won the date yesterday. He asked where I wanted to go. I said come to my room after class tomorrow. He said okay." She blows out a long breath. "And wow. I can't tell you how badly I needed that. Complete stress reliever."

"Who *are* you?"

She grabs her bag of toiletries and smirks. "I'm a satisfied woman who just had her brains fucked out by a big strong man. I highly recommend it. Very beneficial for endorphin production." She strolls by me with a grin and leaves.

I'm completely jealous. Completely. And the only thing I can think of now is what it would be like to be with Hunter. Logically speaking, if everyone thinks we've had sex, what's the harm? Because I'd really, really like to feel as good as Elle looks.

Liar. That's not why you're wondering.

CHAPTER FOURTEEN

That evening, I'm dressed in a short light blue summer dress and white sandals. I can't decide if I really want to play this pretend game anymore, so I only go halfway on the makeup. Remember, Lainey and Jessica are supposed to believe that I caught Hunter simply by playing a part—easy, not so smart, fun. And the original plan for tonight was to demonstrate that I have Hunter—yes, big, ripped from head to toe, Mr. hottie quarterback—at my beck and call, completely whipped. Hunter is fully prepared to play his part so I win the bet and become a Tri-Kapp.

There are only three problems:

One, I cannot get this morning out of my head. The memories, though still foggy, hold just as much meaning as the fact that my brain went to great lengths to shield me from them. It's been eating away at me all day. Why would I choose to forget all this? How is it even possible?

Two, I now question every decision I've ever made, because my unshakable foundation—the assumption that I'm intelligent and/or can think my way through any obstacle—is complete bullcrap. Example: this moment. I can't think my way out of this. Another one: I thought I hated this guy who I believed loathed me for the last thirteen years. He didn't. Not entirely. I misread the situation or didn't want to see what was really going on with him. Did he tease me because he liked me all that time? No. But the assumption that he hated me no longer hunts. (No pun intended.) Twice, he stepped up to protect me. Twice. But that doesn't mean he's in love with me. That doesn't make sense either.

I think...I think he actually sees me almost like a sister or something. I got along with my big brother, but Rachel—my best friend back home—didn't. She always complained about her brother making her life a living hell, but also being very protective.

My stomach curls with the thought. I don't want to be in the sister zone. Mostly because of point number three: I can't stop thinking about how puzzling our relationship was and is, and how he evokes chaos inside me. Mentally and physically. That body—tall, strong, and ripped from head to toe—is nothing shy of masculine perfection. I've seen him enough times with his shirt off, tossing footballs with his dad in their front yard. There's not an ounce of fat to be found on those bulging pectorals or abdominal muscles with grooves so deep they could be mistaken for rain gutters. I remember once looking out my window, thinking how he looked like he'd been cut from angry steel, whatever that means. I can't stop thinking about how it would feel to have those warm, steely ripples sliding over my soft bare stomach, the weight of his strong body over me, his breath mixing with mine.

Add all these things together, and I'm a molten mess. My present doesn't hold the same meaning, my past doesn't hold the same meaning, and my future is basically tied to one giant sinful moment that doesn't make a whole hell of a lot of sense and won't ever happen. With all the pretty fish in the ocean, Hunter would never be into me. Not like I might be into him. It's a crude awakening to be the girl Lainey and Jessica said I was—needy. It's even more harrowing not knowing what to do about it.

For the first time in my life, I'm completely lost.

As I ring the doorbell at the Tri-Kapp House, Hunter takes my hand. It's warm and rough, and I try to ignore those two facts. He hasn't said much since he came by to get me, but I know it's because he's reacting to my coldness.

"Wow. Those are some sweaty palms you got there, sugar rump." He smiles just as the door swings open.

Lainey is dressed like a pink princess in a frilly dress and tiara. I'm sort of speechless and I see

Hunter is, too. Because that is some outfit.

Her brown eyes wash over me with disdain and then move to Hunter. He's looking exceptionally hot tonight in a pair of well-loved button flies, a short-sleeved blue Polo that matches his eyes and a pair of leather flip-flops. Normally, I'd turn my nose up at a guy in beachwear in the middle of Texas, but Hunter has the nicest toes I've ever seen. They're downright beautiful. And with his tall, athletic frame, he looks like Mr. Perfect Boyfriend just out for a casual night with his girl.

Even Lainey, the snob to end all snobs, can't take her eyes off him.

"Eh-hem. Can we come in?" I ask.

Lainey snaps out of her lusty trance. "Ah. Yes. That'll be five dollars per couple. Wait. No. Make that ten because you're an Alpha, which requires additional insurance," she says to Hunter.

Hunter stares at her like she's some ridiculous bug he's not sure what to make of and then reaches for his wallet. "Here's twenty. Keep the change." Slightly limping, he steps inside past her like she's nothing but an opponent on the field he'd sooner push over than speak to.

We immediately see the living room is packed with people getting ready for the movie marathon, piling up on the couch and cushions. Hunter steps forward, and I watch those shoulders square in preparation for his entrance.

Like me, Hunter is not shy. He never has been.

Never will be. And when he walks into a room, he always does the same thing: stops where everyone can see him, makes eye contact with as many people as possible to let them know he's there, and then he cracks that panty-melting smile, which serves two purposes: One, melting panties. Two, signaling to the other alphas in the room they should make friends with him because he's a fucking bigger, badder alpha. Everyone wants to fuck him or be him.

Or both?

I've watched him do this a million different times over the years—usually while I'm sticking my finger down my throat, making a gag sound—but it never ceased to amaze me how effective his technique worked. Only, tonight, we're in my world.

"Wait." I grab his elbow and look up at him. "That won't work here."

He crinkles those perfect straight brows in question.

"Watch and learn." I step past him and enter the room, still holding his hand. I stop in the doorway and several people turn to see who's joined the festivities. I turn to Hunter and hold his hand over my heart. "Listen, Rose. You're gonna get out of here, you're gonna go on and you're gonna make lots of babies, and you're gonna watch them grow."

Everyone claps and laughs, so I take a little bow, not letting go of Hunter's hand. "Thank you. Thank you. My heart will go on." I stand straight and gesture to Hunt. "Everyone, this is Hunter, my Jack Dawson for the evening."

The reception is warm, and I lead him to the back of the room to one of two rows of fold-out chairs. We take the seats on the end, him on the outside.

"What was that?" he whispers in my ear.

"Nerd talk. I'm fluent," I whisper back. Really, it was just the best line from the movie. Anyone with a vagina would know that. And most of the girls here own a copy.

He chuckles softly with that incredibly deep voice that sounds like the Pied Piper's X-rated flute. I don't know how I've overlooked his blatant, sexual magnetism, but now that I'm tuned into his station, I can't seem to shut it off.

"I thought you were supposed to be acting like an airheaded slut tonight," he whispers.

"Oh. Shoot. I forgot." I take my hand, pretend to open up the top of my head and then pluck out my brain and throw it on the floor. "There. All set."

"Okay, babe." He places his strong hand on my thigh. "Just let me know when you want the groveling to begin."

I nod, but look ahead. My body is shaking. *Please don't notice. Please don't—*

"Are you nervous?" Hunter whispers, sounding surprised.

Darn it. "No."

"Hmmm…because I could swear your hand is

shaking."

I snap it away. "I'm just cold."

He smirks. "As is customary when it's ninety degrees outside."

It's not much cooler inside with all of the bodies packed in this room, so he's got me. Yes, again.

"I meant…I just got a little chill. I must be ovulating or something." *Why did I say that?* I look down at the floor, longing for my brain.

"TMI, Tass." He chuckles.

I giggle in a loud, high-pitched voice, pretending like I meant to say it as part of my act. "Oh, Hunter—heeheehee—you're so funny."

He leans in. "I don't think anyone is going to buy a guy like me falling in love with that stoned chipmunk impression of yours."

I frown. "Okay," I say in a low, low voice, "how about a gorilla?"

He wrinkles his nose at me. "You know what? Just let me do all the work tonight. You just sit there and look pretty—something you're good at." He slides his hand up my thigh, and I swear it feels like his fingers are inside my panties.

Within the space of two breaths, I'm aching from his touch. Then there's the fact that he just said I look pretty. He's managed to simultaneously pet my ego and my c-spot, though I'm sure that wasn't his intent. Everyone knows that Hunter's type is blonde, busty, and bubbly. The exact opposite of me. Brunette, budding, and brainy.

I slide his hand away and cross my legs in the opposite direction.

He puts his hand back over the top of my thigh and glides it under the hem of my short dress to where he can practically touch the seam of my panties.

"Stop that," I whisper.

"Oh, but I can't keep my hands off you." He gives my thigh a little squeeze with that big strong hand.

I yelp and jump from my seat.

We're at the back of the room, so only a few people notice.

I look down at Hunter and scowl. "Stop that," I hiss.

He fails at biting back a smile. "Sorry, babe," he says nice and loud, "I just can't help myself. You look too hot in that little dress."

His deep voice elicits attention from the noisy room of approximately fifty people, including Jessica, who's just put the movie on a flat screen mounted to the wall. Lainey is still over in the foyer, greeting people and taking money.

I sit back down with a tight sneer on my lips. He has absolutely no idea what he's doing to me. I'm so turned on that my nipples are poking right through the fabric of my bra and thin dress.

"Wow, Tass. You really are cold." He glances down at my breasts.

I'm going to die. I cross my arms over my chest.

"Eyes up here, big guy."

"Nope. I'm liking the view down there." He continues staring at my chest. "Hey. I can't help if I like looking at you." He lowers his voice. "I just wish you were wearing those big sexy glasses. I kinda have a thing for them."

Huh?

He stands up.

"Where are you going?" I ask, barely able to breathe straight.

"To find you a blanket." He walks along the side of the room, and all female eyes are glued to him. Mine included.

That man makes me hot. Really hot.

One of the sorority sisters seated in front of me turns around. "So is that the Alpha guy you made a bet on with Lainey?"

"Yeah." I'm not surprised she knows. They all do.

"Ohmygod. He's smokin'. No wonder they accused you of being into him."

Well, now I am. How's that for irony?

I shrug as if to say *"Oh well. Watcha gonna do?"*

"I know, right?" she says. "As if any of us would really date a dumb jock like that. I have socks with a higher IQ." She snorts.

My right hand balls into a fist. I absolutely do not appreciate anyone talking about Hunter in this manner. Yes, I get that a handful of days ago, I was no different than her—a hater. But now I know that being better than someone else doesn't come from the brain; it comes from the heart. You can't smart your way to goodness. You just can't.

She goes on, "What's the difference between a paperweight and a football player?" She snickers. "At least the paperweight has a use."

I shoot up from my chair, holding back the urge to tell her to shove it. "I should go look for him. He probably got lost on the way to the bathroom," I say through clenched teeth.

She cracks up. "Good one."

I was being sarcastic, you judgmental sow rectum.

I head from the room to find Hunter. I'm not staying here one more minute and listening to these people slam him. *They don't even know the guy!*

Yes, fine! I'm a hypocrite. But they didn't endure over a decade of suffering with the egotistical man. I earned the right to judge him!

Yet...I never really knew him. Did I?

I stop in the foyer, reeling with anger. Not at the Tri-Kapps, necessarily, but at myself. How could I have ever believed that putting people down like that was okay? What the hell was wrong with me?

I hear Hunter's signature deep voice and follow the sound through a short hallway into the large kitchen. It's one of those open types with a big island in the middle and white cupboards. Lainey's leaning up against the counter in her pink monstrosity, giggling, and Hunter's standing there having some sort of chat with her.

I can't believe this. She's batting her eyelashes and acting all coy. *What a troll!*

"There you are!" I say.

Hunter turns his head. "Hey, babe. I was just chatting with your friend Lainey about—"

"We're leaving," I say.

His smile melts away. "Did something happen?"

I got a wake-up call from the universe. She says it's time to get my head out of my ass. "Actually, yes. But I'll explain on the way back to the dorms."

"Uh, okay." He looks at Lainey. "Nice meeting you."

"Nice meeting you, too," she says in a saucy-minx voice.

I literally want to scratch out her eyes. "I'll meet you outside, Hunter. I need to talk to Lainey for a moment."

He nods stiffly. "Sure."

I wait until he's out of the room before I turn to Lainey with the intention of telling her what a disgusting human being she is, but she starts laughing, hitting her knee.

"Oh my, Tassie. You were totally right. Act a little stupid and like you're desperate for sex, and guys like him are all in."

"What are you talking about?"

"You win. Completely." She holds up her hands. "Welcome to Kappa Kappa Kappa."

"I'm confused."

"What's there to be confused about? Everything you said is true. It isn't hard for girls like us to get a dumb jock like that." She leans in. "I think I might even take him for a ride—teach him a few lessons, if you know what I mean?"

White rage dots my vision. Before I know what I'm doing, my hand is up in the air, cocking back and flying forward with all five digits stretched for action. My palm meets her cheek with such force that her head whips to the side.

"He is *not* a dumb jock, you crack rat," I snarl.

Lainey's brown eyes go wide and she cups her cheek. Within a split second, her face turns fire engine red. "You dirty little dwarf star!" She lunges, and I reach for the neck of her stupid pink dress, yanking it to the side, hoping to throw her off balance. Instead, I just tear the front, exposing her pink bra. Stuffed pink bra. The white tissue pops out like a groundhog on his favorite day.

She gasps and then snarls. "You're gonna die!"

I don't know what I'm doing, my body is in control now, but my fist cranks back, and I pop her right in the boob (padded, so no effect), and she grabs hold of my curly hair.

"Hey! Break it up!" With his strong arms, Hunter pulls us apart like two-year-olds fighting over a toy.

"I'll kill you!" Lainey screams.

"You're too stupid to kill me!"

Hunter pries us apart.

"Get out, and take that bucket of andesite with you!" she screams.

"He is *not* made of lava rocks. He's more like granite. Or fine marble! Don't you see those muscles?" I yell, pointing to Hunter. "The muscles you just told me you wanted to hump?"

Lainey's head jerks back. "I said no such thing!"

"Oh, yes, you did! And you know what, you mealworm brain?" I point my finger in her face. "He wouldn't screw you if you showed up at his door with an extra box of tissue in your bra and a bucket of lube in your hand!"

"Out!" She points toward the door. "You're not welcome here. We don't allow scum like you in our sorority."

"Correction. It's the only thing you allow." I look at Hunter, who's positively amused.

"Let's go," I snap.

He looks down at me and cracks the widest, most beautiful smile I've ever seen. Those dimples underneath his dark stubble are so deep you could park an eco-friendly car in them.

"I'll be right there," he says.

Huh? "I really think—"

"Wait for me outside," he orders.

"Why?" I ask.

He looks into my eyes. "Because you trust me," he says softly.

I do, of course, but that doesn't make his request any stranger.

"Oh, okay." I head for the door, but slow my steps before I actually get to it. Why did he ask me to leave?

Suddenly I hear, "You prick!" ring through the air.

Hunter comes from the kitchen, laughing.

"What was that about?" I ask.

He opens the door. "I told her we stole her vibrator collection the other night, too."

"What?"

He nods. "She had ten."

"No."

"Yes. And she had names on them."

We step outside and shut the front door. "Please tell me you're kidding."

"The biggest one was named Hunter," he says with a giant smirk.

I laugh. And then I laugh harder. The tears form in my eyes, and I can barely breathe, so I bend over.

"You okay?" Hunter pats my back.

"Yeah." I suck in some air. "Never better." I stand up straight and look up at those big blue eyes.

"So you're done with the Tri-Kapps, huh?" he asks.

I nod.

"You sure? Because I was really making some headway with her. She offered to come over and clean my dorm room."

Bitch! It just goes to show that having a high IQ

doesn't mean you're a good person. It doesn't even mean you're smart.

"Yeah, I'm sure," I say.

His smile melts away. "What changed your mind, Tassie?"

I look down at my sandals. How do you tell a guy you've known since you were five, who you've hated for as many years, that you think you might like him? *More than like him.*

I clear my throat and bite the side of my lip. "Let's just say that any club who won't have you isn't good enough for me."

He jerks his head back. "That's a change."

"Sorry?" I thought he'd be flattered.

"How come I'm suddenly good enough for you now, after all these years?"

"You were never *not* good enough for me. What gave you that impression?"

"Everything."

I blink and try to process that. I don't want to say a word because my brain—the smart part—tells me there's more I've blocked out aside from that horrible night over two years ago.

"I-I—"

"Come on. Let's get you home." He takes my hand. His feels warm and rough and safe.

I wrap my fingers around it and nod. "Sure."

CHAPTER FIFTEEN

Hunter didn't say much aside from goodnight when we got to my door. And being that I felt thoroughly adrift in the ocean of angst, I didn't attempt to engage. I said goodnight. He said goodnight. He walked away. I went inside my room.

"What!" I cringed. *Thighs. Boobs. Balls.* "Elle!" I had to scramble from the room again and wait for Elle to finish her stress-relief session. Ten minutes later, Henry emerged with a giant smile.

"Yeah. Yeah," I pffed and went inside.

Elle was fast asleep under the covers, and I got into my PJs. I didn't dream at all, but when I woke, I felt it all bubbling to a head.

I have to tell Hunter how I feel. And I need to know why he spent so much energy and effort hurting me all these years. *And protecting me.* I need to know how he feels. Which is why I'm now sitting in the bleachers after jogging—yes, jogging—me!—around the track at six a.m. on a Saturday morning. By six forty-five, the football team starts filtering in, looking like they've been chewed up and spit out by the margarita blender.

When I finally see Hunter, I jump to my feet and make my way down the bleachers to the side of the field. He sees me almost right away and heads straight for me.

"Didn't expect to see you here," he says, and I can't determine if he's happy or annoyed by that.

"I think we need to talk?" I have no clue why I made that sound like a question.

"All right."

His tone tells me he expected this.

"I have practice for two hours," he says.

"Oh, I thought you'd be sitting it out because of your ankle."

"It's sore, but I'm okay."

"Oh." I look at the ground and an awkward silence sifts between us.

"Later, a bunch of us are going to Henry's folks' cabin near Lake Travis since there's no game this weekend. Why don't you come?" he says.

The tone in his voice isn't funny or flirty. It's serious. Like he's offering something that I should think about before accepting.

But I don't need to think about it.

I nod.

"Good," he says. "I'll swing by your room in a few hours, around ten."

I smile, but I don't feel it. "Sure. Sounds good." I turn to head back to my room, feeling him watch me. I have no clue what he's thinking. I just know we both have a lot we're not saying, and I'm not entirely sure his unsaid words won't smash my heart into a thousand particles.

Please don't land me in the sister zone. Please.

"Hey, Tass!" he calls out.

I stop and turn. "Yeah?"

"Bring your DVD of *Titanic*."

"Why?"

He shrugs. "You didn't get your chick flick last night."

I bob my head. "Uh...sure."

He smiles like he wants to comfort me. Or perhaps he needs some reassurance himself. Maybe we both need it. For sure, this is uncharted waters, but am I really ready for the truth? Is he ready to say it?

Why did you fucking hurt me so badly for over a decade?

My biggest fear is that he'll say something horrible—like "I really hated your nerdy guts and thought it was funny to watch you suffer." I hope that's not his excuse, because this guy? I want to trust him. I want to let it all go and forgive him. But if he can't give me a good reason, then everything I'm feeling only proves that he can be a very sadistic person and that I'm a sucker for having any feelings for him, despite his two acts of heroism.

Just outside the stadium, I close my eyes and tilt my face to the sky. *Please, please, please let there be a reason for all this.*

Something wet slops into my eye and I jerk my

head down. I wipe with my hand, thinking it would just be my luck to have a bird crap on me in reply. I look at my finger. The liquid is clear.

Rain.

I look back up at the random cloud in the sky. "Geez. Thanks." I have no clue what that means.

"You're joking, right?" I ask Elle, who blushes. "You're going to Henry's cabin for the weekend?"

"Just for the night. I'm driving up after I finish a few things; then I'm going to my parents' house tomorrow and won't come back until late Monday."

"So you're skipping classes?" I ask.

"Yeah."

"Everything okay?"

She folds up a pair of jeans and shoves them into her overnight bag. "No. But it's no surprise."

"What happened?" I ask.

"She's dying. It's slow. It's hard on my dad. And me." She smiles, but it doesn't touch her brown eyes. "Can we please not talk about it? I kind of need this space of my life to be separated from it all. Helps me cope."

"Yeah. Of course. Whatever you need."

"Well, right now I need to finish packing and get some work sent off to my professor so it's not turned in late."

"Anything I can forge for you? A brilliant essay

on the principles of quantum string theory, for example?"

She raises a brow. "What decade are you from? *Battlestar Galactica*?"

"String theory hasn't been disproven."

She rolls her eyes. "Like it needs to be," she mutters with a snicker.

"Hey! I'm a bio-E major, not a black-hole whore."

She laughs and throws a sock at me. "You're just a whore!"

I can't help but laugh when she does. It's kind of a little squeak. "Says the girl getting it on with a stupid gorilla."

Her smile melts away.

"I'm so sorry. I was just kidding. Henry's not a gorilla." I should be ashamed of myself for stereotyping him, even if he started that entire bet thing for their scavenger hunt. For which he apologized.

"It's okay." She sighs. "I know I'm overly sensitive about everything lately. I can't help it. But Henry is good for me. He's what I need right now. The opposite of serious."

I get that. "And I don't judge you one little bit. I promise." If anyone deserved to own a tiny hut on the island of fun, it's Elle. She's in emotional-survival mode.

"Thanks." She draws a breath and releases it. "I know it's weird, but everything feels simple with him. We laugh. We talk about stupid things—like movies and school. He's not carrying the weight of the world on his shoulders. He's just…happy. I envy him in a way."

"That's great," I mutter, wishing I had that with someone. "Are you worried about what Lainey will say if she finds out about Henry?"

Elle shakes her head. "Those Kappas give us smart girls a bad name."

"So you're not joining them?"

"Did you see me at movie night?" she asks.

Now that she'd mentioned it, no. But I thought she'd been studying.

She goes on, "I never really wanted to join a sorority, but you said you wanted to and I thought it might be a good way to keep my mind off things while I'm here."

"Then I'm sorry. Because you're right. They're bad PR for intellectual rock stars like us." I grin. "Which is why I'm not joining either."

"Because of Hunter."

"No," I deny, but then start to think about it. "Maybe. But mostly because I don't want anything to do with a group of people who spend their energy being so bitter. What's the point?"

"No point," she agrees.

"Exactly."

"So Hunter." She cocks her head to one side.

"Yes?"

"Was I right about him liking you all these years?"

It's a damned good question. "I don't think that was it."

"Then what?"

"I just don't know, but that's why I'm going." Tonight, come hell or high water, Hunter is going to come clean with me.

"Do you like him, Tass?" she asks while I pack.

"I don't know that either." I shrug. It feels much bigger than "like" to me.

"But you think you might."

"Yeah. I might."

She claps. "This is wonderful! Because I think he'd be good for you."

I am not so sure. "So what about you and Henry?"

She swipes her hand through the air. "Oh, come on. You know he's just for fun."

"How would I know that?"

"Tass, come on. My mom is dying. I'm a wreck fifty percent of the time. What guy would want to deal with that when he's in the prime of his life, getting ready to finish college and play for the NFL?"

"Elle," *how can you be so dense?* "how do you not see how incredible you are?" She's smart and cute and could be described as addictive, like a Rice-Crispy treat. The wide brown eyes and gap-toothed smile make her look like a young Madonna, but with down-to-earth clothes. Add the deep, insightful personality and curvy little body? Super catch. Then take into account that she has the brain power to make anyone feel dumb as a bucket of roach toes, but never, ever does anything other than act supportive and humble? Well… "If you had a penis, I'd totally fuck you."

"That's good to know, because I've been meaning to tell you something."

I stare at her for point five seconds before throwing a shoe at her. "Snot rag!"

"Period hut!"

"Fart bubble!" I throw back.

"Grim reaper fingered aye-aye!"

I couldn't beat a tiny nocturnal creature with skeletal fingers and enormous creepy eyes. "Fine. Point you."

"Ha! I win!" She pauses. "What are we fighting about again?"

"I can't remember. But," I take a deep, deep breath, "I'm happy we're going to Henry's cabin together."

Her expression turns pensive. "Is that because you're planning to sleep with Hunter and feel nervous?"

"I don't know."

"It's okay, Tass." She places her hand on my shoulder. "It's okay to love someone who's not like you."

It's the first time in my life I've ever heard that thought out loud. But sometimes that's what it takes to make something real.

She smiles and then shoves more things into her bag—book, T-shirt, panties. "It's kind of weird, don't you think?"

"What?" I ask.

She shakes her hand at her bag dismissively, like she feels ridiculous. "Nothing…"

"Tell me. What?"

She hesitates. "It's funny that you and I ended up roommates. And we both have a thing for guys that are our complete opposites."

"That's the beauty of the universe. It knows a hell of a lot more than we do." Life is really just one big discovery. Mostly, though, we're just trying to figure out who the hell we are.

I wonder if we ever get there.

CHAPTER SIXTEEN

I text Hunter, telling him that I'd meet him up at the cabin since I want to ride with Elle, and I, too, have a lot to do, starting with calling my mother.

The conversation barely registers in my head as we're speaking. I say I'm not getting into Kappa Kappa Kappa.

She asks why.

I say because they are a bunch of intellectual Nazis spreading hate among the masses and I am not cool with that.

She says I'm exaggerating and being childish, that this is a huge "lost opportunity" because their network reaches into every major university and laboratory in the US.

I say nothing. How can I? How can I explain that the boy next door, from the family they barely speak to because they aren't like my parents or their friends, makes me question everything I've ever wanted?

So I finish the short call, feeling a mixture of emotions. I'm ashamed for not having lived up to

Summerset standards again. But there's also this tiny
tingle of proudness. Bottom line, I've done the right
thing, and though they may not understand it, I do.
It feels good to stand on my own two emotional
feet, and I have a feeling I'm going to be doing a lot
more of it from now on.

I pop down to the student convenience store to
buy a few snacks and drinks for the drive before we
hit the road. The cabin is less than an hour away,
but both Elle and I skipped breakfast. As I'm
standing buying the obligatory road-trip can of
Pringles and Vitaminwaters, the wall of condoms
behind the register starts calling my name. *Hey,
Tassie. Don't be stupid, girl*—they all sound like
Snoop Dogg for some strange reason—*you know you
needs some o' these bad boys.*

"Will that be all?" the cashier—a blonde girl my
age—looks at me with raised eyebrows.

"Oh, uh…yes. That's all." I completely chicken
out. Mainly because it's foolish to think Hunter's
ever going to want me in that way. And if he did,
how incredibly arrogant would I look pulling out a
box of condoms. *Hey, I knew you were feelin' me,
Hunt. So I brought these*—now I'm speaking like
Snoop Dogg, too.

I'm ridiculous. I grab my purchased snacks, but
halfway down the hall, I stop and go back. "I'll take
a box of Magnums." It's an educated guess, because
no guy carries himself like Hunter does without
having something large packed away down there.

Plus, I've seen that bulge.

I throw the condoms in my bag and immediately feel ridiculous again. I know he sees me like a sister, and I know tonight could very well end in a bad place. There's a lot of emotion being held back by walls of scar tissue, and one wrong word from him will open up those floodgates.

He's going to come through, Tass. He's going to have some wonderful reason for the last thirteen years.

But if that were the case, I would've figured it out.

I chuck the box of condoms in the trash.

By the time Elle and I arrive in her car—a white Nissan Cube—it's almost three o' clock on this lovely Saturday afternoon. Henry answers the door in shorts and a plain tee. His enormous body practically takes up the entire doorway. The moment he spots Elle, he has her in his giant arms and is blowing raspberries on her neck. She sort of looks like a child compared to his supersize.

"Stop! You're going to make me pee." She giggles. "And my bladder is full."

Henry laughs. "Oh, does my little sweet pea need to tinkle? Let big strong Henry take care of that." He throws her over his shoulder and marches off down the hall. Elle is laughing, telling him there's no way in hell she's letting him take care of that particular need, but she's got other things he can help with.

I stand there smiling, entranced by the two. They're like a couple of playful puppies (a Mini Yorkie and a Great Dane), and it makes me feel so damned good to see Elle happy. I know her heart needs this.

Carrying my overnight bag, I close the door and make my way down the short hallway toward the sound of male laughter. Hunter, Henry and a few of the guys drove together in Henry's black Cadillac SUV. A text earlier from Hunter mentioned some other girls—his friends'/teammates' girlfriends— would be showing up after cheerleading practice.

"Uh...cabin?" I mutter, my eyes sweeping the interior of the enormous A-frame home with soaring knotted pine ceiling and an interior balcony overlooking the great room. The kitchen, to my right, all granite and stainless steel, is so big it likely requires its own zip code. I know from the layout there's another wing of the house, too.

I step into the living room area, where Hunter and a couple of guys are playing pool and drinking beer.

Hunter's stunning blue eyes lock onto me, and his stare is almost predatory.

My heart squeezes and then pounds away like a war drum. Then my mouth goes dry. He looks especially hot today in a fitted light gray T-shirt that accents his strong chest and arms. He's also got on those faded jeans that show off his powerful legs. His dark hair is cut short and messy, but his jaw is covered in a week's worth of stubble. He looks raw and carnal, like he's put his sexual potency on proud display.

Well, call me a peacock. Because I can't stop looking at his feathers.

Staring like I am, he suddenly smiles and jerks his head like he's caught himself doing something he shouldn't. "Hey, guys. Look who's here."

"Welcome to Casa Walton," one of the guys—big with a shaved head and trimmed beard—says with a beer salute.

Henry's last name is Walton. I vaguely remember mention of a Walton family who owns a heck of a lot of oil wells in Texas. That, or some major shares in Walmart. Either way, this is a getaway mansion, not a cabin.

"Guys," Hunter says, "this is an old friend, Tassie. Elle is her roommate."

They grumble and head-jerk in a friendly way. Hunter introduces them as Mike T., Mike J., and Brian, who's the big guy with the beard. The other two are blond and almost the same height. It's good they're both named Mike because I'd probably get them mixed up.

I make a little wave. "Nice to meet you."

"You want a beer?" Hunter asks.

"Uh, sure." I figure it won't hurt to loosen up those inhibitions a little and get ready for our talk.

"Right this way."

I follow him into the kitchen area, taking a moment to admire the way his broad back tapers down to his tight waist.

"I see you cut your hair," I say, making conversation.

He jerks open the door of the built-in fridge, which is loaded with drinks and snacks. "We have team photos Monday, so the coach told us we had to get cleaned up. I went right after practice."

You look amazing. Without the hair, I can see those sculpted cheekbones and that rigid, powerful jawline. "The team should sell your picture to raise money for charity."

Hunter grabs a Dos XX, pops the top, and hands it over. "Aww...are you saying you think I'm cute, Tassie?"

I bat my eyelashes. "No. You're horrible. In fact, monster is the first word that comes to mind when I see you." I smile.

He throws the beer cap at my chest. "Ditto."

"Ha."

We stand there for an awkward moment staring at each other. Suddenly, all I can think about is that tiny box I left behind in the trash back on campus. Just standing next to him is making my body spark up in sinful places. It's a little sad to discover your erogenous zones at such a late age, but I always say better late than never.

Still, it shocks me that the guy who's been the

catalyst for so much change in my life is this Hunter.

I hold back a sigh. He's so damned beautiful. How come I never saw it before? Those eyes. So blue. So intense with the curtain of dark lashes. When he looks at me, like right now—all serious—it makes me feel like he's decided I belong to him.

"So," he says casually and reaches for another beer before closing the fridge, "what would you like to do first?"

"What do you suggest?" I ask, a hint of flirtiness.

"You like pool?"

"Never played, but how hard can it be? It's just geometry with a stick and ball."

He makes a little chuckle that rumbles deep in his wide chest. "Leave it to you to nerdify the great game of pool." He cracks a big smile.

"Nerdify?" That comment justifies payback. "Well, at least I don't try to make everything into a muscle contest," I tease.

"Hey, when you got guns," he makes a fist and flexes, popping out a half-cantaloupe-size bicep, "gotta find any excuse you can to fire that ammo."

I know he's kidding around. He hasn't been a big show-off since, well, before that one summer.

"Okay," he says, "as soon as the guys are done with that game, you and I can play. I want to see some of that stick math of yours. Why don't I give you a tour in the meantime?"

"Sounds good."

Hunter shows me around—back patio with hot tub, grill, horseshoe pit. There's a movie theater with seating for fifteen and a large garage with a bunch of toys—boat, jet skis, canoes. Hunter mentions that Henry's parents are in fact in the oil business, but don't spend much time here.

We walk down another hallway, and he opens up the door, the first along a well-lit hallway with skylights above.

"And this is your room." He steps inside, and I follow.

"It's really nice." Big bed, fireplace, and there looks to be a nice bathroom, too. I then notice a duffel bag on the bed. It's Hunter's. The name over the Pirates logo says Johnson.

My pulse rate slips into warp speed, and I suddenly feel my heart is going to pop out of my chest and dance around on the floor, possibly doing a striptease or twerking or something shamefully inappropriate.

He must've noticed the freaked look on my face because he throws out, "If you want to stay here, that is. If not, there's another room right down the hallway."

I don't know what to say, so I run my hands over my hair and whoosh out a breath. *Okay. Okay. This is happening.*

Hunter's offering to take my virginity tonight. For real.

The look on his face is as serious as it is carnal. I can see the hunger in his eyes.

I suddenly think about him naked, on top of me, right there in that big bed I'm now eying cautiously.

"Okay." He holds up his hands in the I-surrender position. "I'm sorry I said anything. I'll show you that other room."

He moves toward the open doorway.

"Wait. Just…" I wince, trying to clear my head. "Just wait."

"What?" He sounds angry.

"We have *got* to talk."

"I think you just made yourself pretty clear."

Huh? "About what?" Because I haven't said a damned word yet.

"It's always been like this with you, Tassie. I don't know why I expected it to change."

"What are you talking about?" I ask, because I'm genuinely lost.

"This…thing with you, it's…" He shakes his head toward his feet and places his hands on his sides. "It's fucked up."

I blink, trying to process. "I don't understand. What have I ever done to deserve that *awesome* comment?"

"I'll make it clear for you: You're a stuck-up little snot-nosed snob."

"Snob?" I whisper.

"Yes, you've always looked down your nose at

everyone. Including me. You're like this little carbon print of your parents."

"Whoa. I don't think that I'm better than everyone else," I say, but it's a lie. I know it is.

"Really?"

"Okay, maybe I used to. Maybe I tried to focus on my strengths, but how else was I going to survive all those years of your abuse?"

Hunter's eyes fill with rage. He turns toward the door, and I think he's going to leave, but no. He slams it shut and turns around, preparing to tear me a new one—finger pointed accusatorily, face red, veins popping from his neck.

Jesus. I instinctively step back.

"You," he growls in a low voice, "*you* deserved every bit of public humiliation."

"Ohmygod. Are you out of your mind? You threw food at me. You had the entire school picking on me, making fun of my virginity and the fact I wasn't pretty. You were cruel, Hunter. Fucking cruel to the bone."

"Wrong. I defended you. Repeatedly. Only to be slapped in the face. Then I gave you everything you deserved, Tassie. Because you dished it out twice as bad back to me."

He's out of his thick skull! "What did I do to you?" I bite back.

"Geez, Tass. I don't know," he says like a giant smartass. "You try hearing you're a stupid pea-brained dumb jock from the smartest person in school. And then you try going home and hearing the same bullshit from your father. I had *him* at night and *you* during the day. It's a fucking miracle I didn't jump off a goddamned bridge."

Oh. I feel like I've been punched in the gut. Or that he's pierced my heart with something cold. The pain is immediate, and I can only assume because he's telling me something I know is true.

Was I the aggressor?

That can't be right. I turn, walk over to the bed, and sit on the edge. All these years, I told him he was stupid, worthless. I never imagined he'd been listening.

But he was.

My brain does some acrobatics, pulling together the pieces. I'm starting to think that his lashing out at me was never about me. It was about his father—the guy he couldn't lash out at. But did I really deserve all that?

I swallow. "It doesn't excuse what you put me through, Hunter."

He blows out a breath and drags his hand over his short messy hair. "I know that now, Tass. I know I was a dick and taking out my frustrations on you. And I know that I crossed the lines sometimes, but you always laughed me off. As hard as I pushed or messed with you, you just smiled and told me to fuck off. Or you called me stupid and walked away. I had no idea you ever gave a shit about what I said or did to you. Not until the other day when you told me."

I try to pull it all in and digest, but mostly I'm thinking about how stupid we both were. It would've taken so little to change things. I could've told him how he was affecting me, but I was too proud. I'm now guessing he was in the same boat.

"Well," I look down at my palms, "I'm sorry. Because you're not stupid. I am. I should've known better." I did, after all, live next door to Hunter. I heard the things his father said.

Hunter sits next to me on the bed but doesn't speak for a long moment. "I'm sorry, too."

With hesitation, I glance at him. We made each other so miserable that it's almost comical. Almost. Regardless, I start to laugh.

"What?" he says with a smile.

"You really pushed my buttons. I mean the pranks and the whole 'you're my nerd' thing. You're the king of psychological warfare."

"Well, I'm not going to lie. I did enjoy it. Just a little."

"I think I did, too. I mean, you know—seeing you try so hard to get to me, and then there'd be that whole disappointed look on your face when you didn't get anything."

He bobbed his head. "I think that's why I always liked you so much. Everything just slid right off—nothing bothered you. Everything bothered me."

He was very good at hiding it. "So you wanted

to be like me, is that it?"

"That's pushing it." He grins. "I think I was more interested in dating you—the one girl I couldn't have."

His words shock the hell out of me, and my smile fades.

"Don't look so surprised, Tassie. I hinted at it enough times."

No. No, he didn't. Or, at least, he wasn't speaking my geeky language. "I always thought you were joking."

"Would you have acted differently if you'd known I was serious?" he asks.

"I don't know," I answer honestly. It all feels so long ago, and I feel so different.

"And now?"

It takes me a long moment to work up the courage to answer him. I turn my head and look him in the eyes. "Now I can't see wanting anyone *but* you."

"I feel the same way, Girl Back Home." The corner of his lip curls into a sinful, cocky little smile. "Can I kiss you now?"

So it was me. All along. "Oh God, yes."

His mouth is on mine fast. His kiss is rough and raw, packed with emotion. I place my hand on the side of his face, drinking in the male texture of his short stubble. I open up to him, allowing his tongue to slide over mine and tangle and lap. He tastes like I imagined he would, sweet and delicious. It's my first real kiss, and I realize that had it been with anyone else, it would not have been this good.

His lips push and slide over my mouth, and the energy and emotion pour out of me. I can't ever remember wanting something so bad.

His strong arms snake around my back and pull me closer. His tongue goes deeper. The heat floods between my legs, and all I can think about is how much I want him to use that powerful, masculine body of his to relieve the pressure.

"I want to fuck you," he pants in between searing hot kisses. "Right now."

I surmise he's asking permission. He's got it.

I pull back from his sensual lips and whip my T-shirt off. He looks at me for a moment—at my eyes, neck, and chest. "You're so fucking beautiful."

I smile. It feels better than I ever imagined to hear him say that.

He reaches out and slides the strap of my bra down my shoulder and then the other, exposing my bare breasts. "Really sexy."

He pushes me back on the bed and stands.

The shirt comes off, and I want to moan. The endless ripples of rock-hard abs and those rails of muscle running along the inside of his hips are unreal. He's more ripped than I remember.

"Unbutton your pants," he says.

I slowly slide my hands down and do as he asks.

"And the zipper," he adds, so I do that, too.

He grabs hold of the legs of my jeans and pulls down, leaving me in just my panties.

He stares hungrily at the apex between my legs, and suddenly I wonder what I've got on.

I look down. *Shit. Saturday Hello Kitty? Really, Tass. Couldn't even manage some plain old respectable bikini briefs?*

"Wow. Now *those* are sexy," he says with a smirk.

I laugh. "Glad you like them. I've got the whole week. Play your cards right and I'll let you see them."

He laughs and then reaches for the front of those jeans. From the first pop of a button, I can see the dark, coarse hair inside. Another pop and the base of his cock.

I am transfixed by the raw maleness of his body and the immediate sexual need it provokes.

He slides down his pants, not showing any shyness over standing naked in front of me. I can't look away. His cock is thick and long and perfectly pink. It has much more girth than I'd imagined.

"Oh-okay...?" I swallow down a dry lump in my throat, feeling excruciatingly aroused by the thought of him being inside me.

He climbs onto the bed, straddling one knee between my legs, and then dips his head. He places a lingering kiss right over my panties on top of my throbbing c-spot. "You smell so sweet." He kisses me again. "I wanted to taste you so badly the other day in the library, I had to jerk off right after that."

His face had been pretty damn close to everything down there, but who knew he'd been having dirty little fantasies about it?

The thought turns me on so much that my nipples harden to tight little pebbles. I'm too shy to ask him to suck on them and relieve the tension.

Hunter slowly peels down my underwear and then sucks in a breath. "Fucking hell. I think I'm going to come just looking at you." He takes his fingers and gently spreads me. I don't know if this is what guys like to do, but if just looking at his abs and cock and balls turns me on, I'm guessing it's the same for a guy. They just want to see it all.

He bends his head once again and places a soft kiss right over my clit. I gasp and grab fistfuls of the comforter. I've never felt anything better. I can't stop panting. I think I might explode or die of a heart attack if he doesn't make me orgasm in the next ten seconds.

"Just do it. Get it over with," I pant.

He looks up from my groin with a mischievous smile. "Ohellno. I've waited fucking years for this."

He slides partly off the bed so he's kneeling down there and removes my panties along the way. "Come here." He grabs hold of my calves and drags me down so my valley is fully exposed and in his face. "That's better."

He pushes his mouth between my legs and starts kissing and licking. The warmth and pressure are too much, and the tension inside my core shoots through the roof. I can even feel my skin tighten around my bones.

I reach for his head and grind into him, pushing my hips rhythmically, in sync with his tongue. "Fuck, fuck. Oh God. I'm going to…" My voice fades into nothing and my body snaps and releases. Everything lights up with sinful waves of hard, hot euphoric contractions. Just as I'm coming, groaning hard, he slides a finger inside me. It stings. I just don't care. I want him deep. I want more. I never want this to stop.

He milks my climax with his skillful tongue and penetration. All I can do is pant his name.

After several long moments, I feel my body relaxing and floating back down to earth. He pulls his hand away and places one last kiss right over my now hypersensitive bud.

I wince, but it still feels good.

"You need a minute?" he says in that deep husky voice.

I look down at him halfway off the bed, kneeling between my knees. "I don't know. I can't think."

"Neither can I. You're so sexy, Tass. I've never wanted anyone like I want you."

I blink at him. It's a sweet thing to say. "Are we going to…have sex now?" I ask.

"Yes."

I draw a breath. I know what he just did down there was to prepare me, make it less painful. But it's still a little harrowing. He's not a small guy.

"Okay. I'm ready." I scoot back on the bed and grab my T-shirt, putting it underneath me. I feel weird doing that, but I'd feel worse explaining to Henry why I've ruined his comforter.

Hunter stands up, grabs his jeans, and fumbles with something. His back is to me, so I can't see what he's doing. But I do see his perfect ass and him chucking the black and gold wrapper on the floor.

I knew it! Magnums.

He climbs back up onto the bed and lays himself between my legs. His body is heavy and hot. I love how his soft skin and hard muscles feel against mine.

"Are you ready?" he asks.

"Does a koala have fingerprints?"

"Huh?" He frowns.

"Yes. Yes. I'm ready."

He bows his back and places the tip of his cock at my entrance. "Just relax."

I do. I lay my head back, wanting to remember this moment, the sensation of his skin, the sound of his breath.

He thrusts, and I gasp. It hurts worse than I expected, but it also feels so much better too. I let out a soft moan.

"You good?" he asks.

"Yeah, just give me a minute."

He pulls out slowly and then slides back in at a torturously slow pace. My body just wants him deeper. The need to have him move and push is animalistic. It's like no other.

Our mouths press together in wild, hot searing kisses, tongues dancing. His body works over mine—strong shoulders, back, hips—driving his cock deep inside me. His hands are on my breasts, his balls are slamming into my base, his breath is mixing with mine.

I reach under his arms and press my fingertips into his back, pulling him deeper and wrapping my legs around him. I claw at him to get everything.

The erotic sensation builds again, but this time there's more. It's starting from the center of my womb and spreading out through my back and hips and legs. He thrusts hard, and then I'm coming.

"Hunter. Oh God." I pant. "Don't stop."

He doesn't. He uses that strong body to fuck me into the next hemisphere. I claw at his muscled back and then feel his body tighten. He opens his eyes and looks at me for a moment, like a hesitation. But then he can't stop himself. He's watching me come. He's watching me crumble into a million pieces beneath him.

He pumps again—harder, more savage this time—and comes with me. I feel his cock twitch inside as he jets his cum. The sensation drags another orgasm right out of me. The thought of him ejaculating is nothing shy of erotic. Mindless, carnal, and erotic.

I move my hips into him, unable to stop the addictive bliss from feeling our two bodies joined.

He thrusts one final time and then lets out a deep guttural sound. I widen my legs and take him deep, flexing around him, milking him. I love him inside me and how he fills me.

Without pulling out and still panting, he dips his head and places a slow kiss on my mouth. "Please tell me you liked that," he whispers.

I don't have a clue how to process what just happened. It's a lot. It's a lot. *Hunter just fucked me. My first time.* It was great. He'd done everything right and made me feel sexy and beautiful and wanted. I don't think I can ever want anyone else like I want him, and it's terrifying.

"Tass?"

I realize he's still inside me with his elbows propping him up.

"Yeah?"

"Was it okay?" he asks again.

"Completely."

"Good." He kisses me lazily. "Because I think I'd like to do that again."

He can't be ready already, I think. "So soon?"

"It's a first for me. But maybe my body wants to make up for lost time."

I smile at him and brush my fingers over his brow. I still have so much to say and process about us, but right now I simply want to be with him. He and I are finally on the same team, and I suddenly wonder if we weren't all along.

CHAPTER SEVENTEEN

The rest of the evening is a complete blur. Hunter and I have sex once more in the bed—slow and soft. Then we take a shower together. I've obviously never bathed with a guy before, but I quickly come to realize how sensual it is. I love sliding my soapy hands over the hard curves of his ass and arms. I love feeling his naked chest against my bare breasts. I will never shower alone again as long as he's around.

After the shower we talk a little. Mostly he's just apologizing for hurting me. I do the same. Then I feel like this enormous weight has been lifted from my body and soul.

Then, slowly, his eyes start to close. "You feel good in my arms, Tass," he mumbles right before dozing off.

I smile and snuggle into his smooth warm chest. "Ditto." He's left me raw, thoroughly worked over, and one hundred percent feeling like I'd been saving myself for this. With anyone else, it would've been sex. But with him, it was...intense. He made me feel like no one else mattered.

We fall asleep, but it doesn't take long for my body to call. I need to pee. I need water. I need food. In that order.

With Hunter sound asleep, his Adonis-like frame under the covers, I take care of business and then head to the kitchen in my pajamas in search of hydration and nourishment.

Every ounce of my being glows. He's brought me into a mental state where I clearly see what I want and who I'm meant to be. Not a girl looking for approval, but a young woman taking her place in life.

I am almost to the kitchen when I hear my name spoken, then Hunter's.

"Dude, seriously? I wouldn't bang *that* for a Super Bowl ring," says a deep voice.

"Mike, you're a dick," says a girl I don't recognize.

"Yeah," says another girl. "You're being a pig."

"Hey, I'm not the one fucking a geek for points," the voice says.

For a moment, I'm thinking they're talking about Elle and Henry. But then...

"Well, maybe Hunter really likes her," says one of the girls.

"Or maybe he's just a competitive asshole who bangs virgins because he can't stand to lose," says one guy.

"Dude, that's what makes him an awesome

quarterback. He'll do anything to win. He even told everyone that he'd have proof after tonight."

"That's nasty," says one of the girls.

"How else are we gonna know he did it with a real virgin?" says the guy.

What the fuck?

I stop in my tracks and cover my mouth, holding back a horrible sound that might be a scream or might just be a sob. Either way, I keep it at bay. My pride won't let me weep or feel like this. I throw up a mental wall of pure anger. One half goes to me for allowing myself to be suckered like this. The other half goes to Hunter for taking things so far. I gave myself to him. I opened my heart to him. And it was nothing but another bet?

I can't believe it. Really I can't.

But then I endure five more minutes of listening to the conversation. The things these guys have done to score points is deplorable. Breaking windows on cars, stealing exams from professors, banging Gammas (as many as possible), and then there's me. The top of the list. Bagging the unicorn, which is code for fucking the virginal Tri-Kapp with absolute proof. Technically I'm not a Tri-Kapp anymore, but they talk about how he still gets the points because I dropped out of the sorority because of him.

I'm sickened by what I hear, but I'm more sickened by my gullibility. Because what this all means is that Hunter lied to me. It was never enough for him to simply *tell* people we slept together, as he led me to believe, and I agreed to. He really, actually, genuinely needed to do the deed.

That's what this was all about—him asking us to team up and help each other. He only wanted to use the time to convince me to really sleep with him.

Now everything makes sense. The looks, the flirting, the playing nice. He did it all to fool me into believing he actually cared.

All for this. To win a contest.

I want to hurt Hunter for this cruelty and yet, I only have myself to blame. I am the goddamned ignorant child who trusted him.

I turn around and look for the master suite. I think it's down the other hallway. I press my ear to the door and hear deep snoring. It has to be Henry.

I open the door and whisper Elle's name.

After a few moments I hear her. "Tass? Everything okay?"

"No. Can you take me home—I mean, back to campus."

There's a rustle of blankets, and then she's there, stepping out into the hallway. "What happened?" she whispers.

"I-I can't talk about it." I look down at my feet.

She grabs my arm. "Did he hurt you?"

"What? No. I mean…yes. But not like that."

"Then how?" She scowls.

"It was all a joke, Elle. He only wanted me here

for that scavenger hunt."

"No."

"I just heard everyone talking about it." My hands tremble with rage just from saying it.

"But wasn't that part of your deal with him— telling everyone you slept together?"

I shake my head. "He only said that to get me to trust him. He had to *really* sleep with me and provide proof to get the points."

She covers her mouth. "Oh God. Are you sure?"

I nod.

"I'm so sorry. Okay. Get your stuff. I'll be out to the car in three minutes." I hear her grumble something about never forgiving Henry. Obviously, he knew. Perhaps inviting Elle here was only to make me feel more comfortable. I don't know, but I can't put anything past them. I'm thoroughly disgusted. I'm hurt. I'm never going to forget this moment.

Elle and I quietly slip out of the house, and an hour later we're at the dorms. She says she'll sleep here and leave early for her parents' house.

By three a.m. her phone is ringing off the hook. It's Henry asking why she left. "Because you're a disgusting pig. That's why!"

By five a.m. my phone is ringing, too. It's Hunter. I don't answer. I just block. I don't want to hear any more lies. I don't want to hear any more bullshit.

He's won. I'm just some stupid geek who

thought she was smarter than the rest and took a leap of faith for once in her life.

A mistake I'll never make again.

The rest of Sunday morning, I don't leave my bed. My body is sore and a reminder of last night with Hunter—a memory I don't want to have. By noon, my mind starts wreaking havoc on me with all sorts of questions—what am I going to do when I see him again? Because I don't want to. Not ever. And while I may be able to avoid him on campus, our parents live next door. There are holidays and summer breaks when we both go home. And, finally, there's my stupidity of bailing out on the Tri-Kapps. Or maybe that wasn't so stupid. Either way, they were right to judge Hunter. Lainey knew all along the sort of low, horrible cruelty these guys are capable of.

Around one o'clock, Elle has already gone to her parents, and I decide I've got to get out of my room for a few hours. I've got to clear my head because I can't permit Hunter or this situation to take more from me than it already has. Last night proved how vulnerable I am, that not facing my feelings has left me weak in some ways.

I go for a drive in my silver Prius, a used one my parents bought me last year. I've already concluded that part of the problem is how I've neglected such a big part of myself—the part of me that wants to be intimate. Science tells us how this is a biological need, and I've been starving myself to a point of stupid desperation.

Yes, that's the solution. I'm going to start dating. Nice, normal, smart guys.

I pull up to my spot in the student garage and let out a big sigh. I feel so heavy inside. I feel so ashamed of myself for letting Hunter fool me.

I slide out my phone and call Rachel, my best friend from back home who's now studying at Harvard. I need to hear her voice.

She answers, and I start to sob.

"Tass? Ohmygod, what's the matter?"

"Nothing." I sniffle. "I just really miss you."

"Oh, sweetie… What happened? Just tell me," she says.

"I can't."

"Why not? You know I love you. Do I need to come there? I'll come there. I'm sure there's a flight or something—"

"I slept with Hunter," I blurt out.

"Oh." She sounds shocked.

"He lied to me and got me to trust him and it was all just some game for his fraternity." My voice sounds all shaky.

"Oh, God. Really?"

"Yeah." I don't want to get into the whole story about him and me agreeing to help each other out by telling a few white lies and pretending to be together. It doesn't really matter in the end. "He played me."

"Oh no. I'm so sorry, Tassie. But you two—you just couldn't ever let it go. I never understood it. The rivalry, the relentless picking on each other."

"*He* picked on me."

"*You* egged him on. But still, this is low, Tassie. Really low. Even for Hunter. I had no idea you two were even talking."

"Yeah, well, it's a long story."

"Whatever it is, it's time you let this thing with him go, Tassie. Just walk away. Move on. For your own sanity."

I know she's right. I can't undo last night. I can't. And I don't have it in me to hate anymore. It's too exhausting. "That's what I'm planning to do."

"Good. And when you see him again, you just lift your chin. Show him that he can't break you. He's just a dumb jock who won't amount to anything."

There was never any love between Rach and Hunter or his posse back in high school. She'd been the recipient of far too many sandwich bombs during lunch.

"Thanks, Rach." I don't feel better, but I do feel clearheaded.

"I can look at flights for next weekend if you want? My mom has miles saved up for me."

"No, I'm okay. I just needed to hear your voice.

That's all."

"I'm here anytime—just call. And please do call. I'm so sick of studying. I think I'm going to go crazy."

"I will." I nod even though she can't see me.

"See you at Thanksgiving, then?"

"Yes, we'll do our girls' day," I mumble.

"Yeah! I love those." She goes quiet for a moment. "Tass?"

"Yes?"

"How was it?" she asks.

"What?"

"Sleeping with him."

I shrug and stare out the window of my car. It's a beautiful sunny day, but everything feels gloomy, like I have rain clouds inside me.

"It was painful," is all I can say, but I mean it in the emotional sense. "Why?"

"I met someone. I'm thinking it's time."

"Oh." I'm happy for her. She's never met anyone she's seriously liked. "Is he in a fraternity?"

"No."

"Then I have no advice to offer other than have a nice time and bring condoms. Lots of condoms."

"Noted." She draws a long breath. "So was there anything good about it all?"

Now that I know why she's asking, I don't want to discourage her from being with someone she has special feelings for, so I set aside my own personal train wreck of emotions. Still, I refuse to say how incredible the sex had been with Hunter or how we moved together so perfectly.

"I don't know..." I sigh. "I guess there were a few moments where it wasn't completely horrible. He took his time making me feel comfortable." My heart cramps with the thought of how he'd made everything perfect for me. Even after, when we were lying there, the conversation we had felt so intimate. He talked about this feeling he had after he almost killed that guy. Life had given him a second chance not to be that person who walked around angry all the time. He said that while it didn't help him figure out who he was, it helped him figure out who he wasn't. I remembered how anytime he looked at me after that summer, I could see it in his eyes—something going on in there. I told him I was sorry he went through all that for me and that I never said thank you.

"Why do you think you didn't remember?" he'd asked.

I can only guess that my severe aversion to violence made me block it out. I doubt I'll ever really know for sure why I forgot.

"I'm not sure," I'd said, "but I remember now. So...thank you."

He'd held me for a while after that, and for a brief few moments, I felt like he loved me. I could see us being happy and good for each other. Yeah, I think that was my favorite part. Feeling completely content and loved for a few short moments before the balloon popped.

I clear my throat, realizing Rach is still there on the other end of the phone. "Just…don't mistake sex for love, Rach. Even if it feels like it, it's not."

CHAPTER EIGHTEEN

When I get back to my room, there's a note on the floor inside the room.

Hunter. He must've slid it under the door.

I stare at the thing, thinking long and hard about what Rach said. This thing—whatever it is between Hunter and I—it's gone on long enough. It's caused me too much pain. And I know whatever the note says, it will only pull me in again. Perhaps it says he's sorry. Perhaps it's a note gloating over his victory. I don't know. But either way, the note contains words I don't want to hear or read. He thinks it's okay to belong to a group that condones this sort of behavior. Well, it's not. He thinks my body is a game piece he can just move around in order to win. Well, it's not.

I stare at the folded paper in my hand for a long time and am about to tear it into tiny pieces, but stop.

"Fucker." I open the thing and read the first two lines.

Tass,

I know why you are upset and angry. Henry spoke to Elle. I'm not going to lie to you and deny the truth. Last night, sleeping with you, it was all part of the bet. But I—

"Asshole!" I tear up the paper and throw the pieces out the window. Whatever else he has to say in this letter is irrelevant. There is no "but." There is no excuse or amount of sorrys—if he's even sorry. There are no words that could possibly make this better.

As I watch the pieces flutter down the side of the building, spreading with the wind, it almost feels cleansing, like I'm letting him go. It's the only way for me to keep breathing.

For the rest of the week, I steer clear of my room and go to the cafeteria at times I know Hunter will be in class or at practice. When I'm not in class, I stick to places I'm unlikely to run into him: the lab, my study group, or at the library on the top floor near the back where it's quiet and I can't be seen. When I'm in my room, I don't answer the door. Someone has come by a few times late at night, knocking. It's either Henry or Hunter. Neither are welcome.

Elle mentions several times that Henry has

texted and wants to see her, but she ignores him and then finally blocks his number. I don't know if she's doing it for herself or in support of me, but either way, I'm grateful not to see any Alphas in my room. They only see me as the nerdy girl Hunter fucked for points. It didn't seem to matter when it was a lie and I wasn't emotionally vested in him, but then it all got real. It all mattered.

On Friday, while I'm in line at the cafeteria, I hear a few guys talking about the big game with Indiana on Saturday. I couldn't be more relieved. The football team will be on the road and that means Hunter won't be around this weekend at all. I know I can't avoid seeing him forever, but I need time to heal and gather my strength. Then, when the time comes, I'll be able to smile and let him know that he may have won, but he hasn't broken me.

The following week, I'm finally feeling a little less fragile. I think I'm almost ready to start taking big steps in my life to address some issues, mainly my reluctance to date anyone. I know part of the problem is that I never felt sexy or dateable. I just felt awkward, like a nerdy little girl in a grown-up body.

But I'm going to change all that. There are plenty of nice, smart guys in my classes. One in particular, Jared, is in my chemistry study group. He smiles a lot and has nice eyes. I think I'll ask him out. I've got to start somewhere.

❦ ❦

Two weeks go by, and it's starting to feel like a bad dream that never happened. All of it.

But then, as I'm walking across the common, heading to class, I see him. It's the middle of the afternoon and those blue, blue eyes are unmistakable. He stops walking and so do I. We just stand there twenty yards apart, facing each other as people pass us. My heart explodes with adrenaline, and I'm fueled with the urge to punch him right in the nuts.

No, Tassie. Don't do it. Don't get sucked in again. I draw a breath and hunker down. I know I have to let go and move on.

I square my shoulders, lift my chin, and walk toward him. He decides to approach me, too.

"Hey," he says calmly, but with an edge to his voice. Maybe he expects me to yell at him. I won't. "How have you been?"

I shrug and put on a friendly smile. "Good. Just busy with school."

He stares for a moment. "Why haven't you returned any of my calls?"

I'm not sure what he expected from me. "Like I said, I've been really busy. But it's nice seeing you." I step around him to head on my merry way.

"Hey." He grabs my hand. "We need to talk."

I frown and pull it away. "What would be the point? You got what you wanted." I allow my eyes to wash over him, like he's my favorite piece of meat. "And I sure as hell got what I wanted." I wink. "Let's call it even."

The confusion is visible on his face—brows knitted together, pulsing jaw muscles.

"Oh, Hunter, what did you think was going to happen? That we'd date or something?" I laugh. "That's funny."

I watch his confusion turn to anger, and now that I taste blood, I want to finish him off. I'm winning. I'm making him feel small, like shit, and it feels good.

I'm about to tell him that a smart girl like me would never date a dumb jock like him, but as I open my mouth, I quickly pull myself back. I don't want to fall back into old painful patterns. I really just want to move on.

"Hunter, we're adults now. You have your life. I have mine. It's time to put the past behind us." I reach out to touch his arm. "Good luck with everything. I mean that." I step around him and continue on my way. My chin is high, but for once it's not because I made him feel worthless, but because I didn't. I've finally grown up a little. I'm finally learning.

CHAPTER NINETEEN

Two Months Later

"You sure you don't want to spend a few days at my house?" I ask Elle as we finish loading up our suitcases with what's essentially dirty laundry to take home for Thanksgiving week. We both live about two hours away, but she's in the opposite direction. Things with her mother remain unchanged, and I don't know if that's good or bad. I try not to push her and instead focus on being there as a distraction. Over the past few weeks, we've gone to a few gatherings (low-key, non-Greek parties with classmates), the movies, and we started jogging a few times a week. I kind of like it. I've even gone on a few dinner dates with that guy Jared. We talked and had a nice time. That was about it.

"I'm sure," she says. "We have a lot of family coming from out of state, so it won't be as difficult as usual."

My heart just cries out for her. "Okay, well, if you feel like you need a break and want to spend a couple of days with me, you're welcome. Our family is local, so we'll have plenty of room in the house. No other visitors aside from my brother."

"Are you going to see your neighbor?"

My stomach twists into a tight ball. I know I'll likely bump into Hunter, and I'm not looking forward to it.

I throw a pair of dirty socks into my suitcase. "I'll ignore him. Just like old times."

Her expression turns heavy all of a sudden—brows furrowed, lips flat. "You know, Tass, I didn't want to tell you this and upset you. I mean—you've worked hard to get over everything and I didn't want to start flicking off scabs."

"What?" I stop packing.

"I talked to Henry a few weeks ago—well, maybe it was a month or so ago. And it wasn't so much talking but begging. On his part."

Ouch. "And?"

"He, Hunter, and a couple other guys got an apartment off campus. I think Henry's paying for most of it, but they're all living together."

That wasn't what I expected her to say. "Nice for them. They can smell each other's farts while they jerk off to pictures of themselves."

Elle's face crinkles up.

"Sorry." That was a bit crude.

"Well, Henry says they left the Alpha fraternity. He said the other guys on the team gave them shit about it, but the whole thing that happened with you really fucked with Hunter's head, so he quit. And then Henry decided he didn't want to be a part of it either. Since then half the guys on the team bailed the fraternity."

I'm stunned. Completely stunned. "I guess…that's good, but—"

"But it doesn't undo their stupidity?" she says.

"Exactly."

"It's a start," she points out.

Maybe. At the very least, the Alphas might decide that losing half their members and the star quarterback is a sign that they need to grow the hell up.

"So does this mean you've forgiven Henry?" I ask.

"We went out a few times—you know, just to talk and hang out, but then I ended it for good. I've got a lot on my plate."

I'm not surprised she didn't tell me that she'd been seeing him again. I probably would've felt betrayed. Now, I'm not so sure I'd care because he made her laugh and she needs as much happiness as she can get.

"It's too bad," I say. "I mean—you seemed happy with him."

She shrugs. "It was a fling. Flings are supposed to be fun. And then they're over."

I really wouldn't know. "I guess."

"Anyway, Henry asked me to talk to you. He wanted me to try to convince you to give Hunter a chance."

"A chance for what?"

"Henry says you don't know everything. That you should at least listen to what Hunter has to say."

I've worked really hard to move past all this. "I don't think it's a good idea."

"That's what I said. Let sleeping dogs lie."

"You were right. My dog's asleep, and I plan to leave it snoring in the corner. Besides, he admitted doing it. What's there to know?"

She shrugs again. "You'll have to ask Hunter that."

Coming home after so many months is far less of a big deal than I'd made it out to be. I sort of expected my room to have been turned into a yoga cave or book room for my parents—those two own a lot of freaking books—but everything's almost the same as when I left, with the exception of my parents being a bit more excited to see me compared to if I were just coming home from school on a normal day.

"Tassie!" My mom throws out her arms the moment I enter the house, which is your typical two-story, stucco ranch built in the '90s. My mother gives me a big squeeze. She looks like an older version of me but with short brown hair and brown eyes. My eyes are blue like my dad's. Both my parents wear thick glasses and stay slim because they forget to eat. They live to work, not work to live.

"Hi, Mom." She lets me go, and I inhale the sweet scent of cinnamon and bread and something roasting in the oven. My mouth waters. "What are you cooking?" The house already smells like Thanksgiving dinner, but that's still five days away.

"Oh, it's a new cleansing diet your father and I are doing. Stewed curried prunes with lentils."

Ewww...

"The chili pepper and cardamom help boost the body's circulation and immune system while the insoluble prune fiber nourishes the probiotic community living in your lower intestinal track."

Yep. Home sweet home. "Is Kyle here yet?" Kyle is my older brother, the tech start-up millionaire. He is also a workaholic.

"He just called and said he's hung up on some new software launch. He'll try to be here late tonight." She swipes her hand through the air. "But if I know him, he won't really be here until Wednesday." My mother smiles, and I know this makes her happy. In her mind, being a workaholic is called being dedicated. She's *very* dedicated.

"Is that my little Sassie Tallahassie?" My father's deep voice rings out from the living room, which doubles as a third study. The first and second studies are the spare bedrooms my parents turned into home offices. But since they ran out of shelf space, the living room now looks like the public library with wall-to-ceiling bookshelves that block out any natural light. It's like a paper coffin. Don't get me wrong. I love books. But deciding that a window is taking up valuable book space, so you block it out with shelving, is a little extreme. Personally, I like sunlight.

"Hi, Dad." I give him a big hug and notice he feels thinner. "Have you lost more weight?"

I pull back and notice how his khakis are sort of hanging off his frame, as is his button-down checkered shirt.

"New project!" he says, sounding all excited.

"You know your father," says my mom. "Just can't get him away from that computer."

Except when it comes to erecting new shelving. I notice they covered another wall, blocking the doorway between the living room and the kitchen. Now you have to go out into the hallway and around.

"Oh, by the way," my mom says, "Hunter was just here asking about you. Something about some assignment from school? I didn't know you had any classes together."

That's kind of strange. And a little intrusive. He knows I don't want to see him.

"We don't. I just help him out once in a while with math," I lie.

My mother shakes her head. "I don't know why you waste your time, Tassie honey."

"What's that supposed to mean?" I ask.

"Well, he's never been very nice to you. I see no reason you should go out of your way to help him when there are plenty of other people in this world who might benefit from your gene pool."

I love how my mother always refers to our gene pool as if we were royalty or saints who perform miracles. In a way, that's the sort of parental brainwashing that messed me up.

"Well, Mom, someone has to take pity on the less fortunate," I say sarcastically.

"Tassie, I'm just pointing out the obvious." She gives me that look, the one that shuts me up unless I'm in the mood to fight, which I'm not.

"Well, I'll go get my stuff from the car and see what he wants." I turn for the door.

"Okay," says my father, "but hurry back. I want to tell you all about this new algorithm we've developed. It has made our climate-prediction model point-zero-zero-five times more accurate."

Oh no. He's going to talk coding. I can't stand coding. It's so binary. "Sounds great, Dad."

"Oh, then I'll tell you about a new study we've just gotten approved by the FDA," my mother adds. "It's cutting edge."

"The monkey nut trial?" I ask.

"Testicles, Tassie. Monkey testicle. But yes."

Now we're talking! I can talk monkey nuts and DNA sequencing all day long.

"Can't wait." I head outside to my Prius and

pop the trunk. I see Hunter's red Mustang in the driveway. His parents gave him that car on his sixteenth birthday and Hunter treats it like his child, always washing and waxing it. Okay, people don't wax children—not that I'm aware of, anyway—but you get the gist.

I stare at the neighbors' front door, thinking about going over and knocking, but I really can't stand seeing his parents. His dad is gruff and loud and his mom never speaks up, not even to defend her own son. They piss me off. They piss off my parents, too, but I think it's mostly because they'd tried to talk about the "Hunter situation," as it was referred to at my house in the early years, but couldn't get anywhere. I would come home crying from elementary school because Hunter did something. My mother would go and try to talk to his father, who would just say something arbitrary like "kids will be kids." As time went on, I stopped crying because I didn't like seeing my parents so upset. However, I think they still knew there were problems, because to this day, they cannot stand Hunter's parents. His folks aren't very nice to us either.

I decide it's better to unblock his number from my phone and text him rather than go over there. I'll tell Hunter I'm busy tonight with something, but maybe we can talk later. Like next year or something.

I lug my giant hot pink suitcase inside—it's

girly and ideal for spotting in any airport baggage claim when I travel—and head straight to the laundry room off the kitchen. I flip on the lights and am surprised there are no books in here.

I set up the first load and then dig my phone from my jeans pocket. As my finger reaches for "unblock" next to Hunter's name, I hesitate. Not about unblocking him, but about what I want to say. Frankly, I just want him to leave me alone and that includes not having to think about what he wants all week long.

I hit unblock and then call. It rings a few times, and I hear that voice. So deep. So familiar. So sexy. It sends prickly goose bumps down my arms and neck, which completely irritates me. One would think after all this drama, my body would know better.

"Tassie?"

"Hey, I just got here to my parents'. What did you need?"

"Can I see you?"

"I'm really busy, Hunter. What do you want?"

"I want to talk."

I think about it for a moment. It feels too painful to move backwards. Forward, away from him, feels right. "I don't think that's a good idea. And frankly, I didn't come home to see you. I'm here to be with my family."

"Tass, I'm only asking for a few minutes of your time."

"Understood. However, I don't owe you anything."

"Also understood," he replies curtly.

"Then why are you acting like I do? Owe you, I mean?"

"I'm not acting; I'm asking. Big difference."

I want to put this behind me, so if he'll drop it, I can spare a few minutes. "I'm having dinner with my parents and then I have plans."

"Fine, then. Let's meet for breakfast," Hunter says.

"I'm jogging in the morning."

"You?" He sounds like he's about to laugh but doesn't.

"Yes. Me."

"Sorry, it's just you were never really into fitness."

"Your point?" He better not be insinuating that I'm fat merely because my body boasts womanly curves. I'm not an athlete. I never will be. *There is fluff in my trunk, and I feel no shame.*

"Just stating a fact. So why don't I join you?" he says.

I think about it for a moment. "Okay. Meet me out front at seven."

"P.m. or a.m.?"

"A.m.," I snap.

"I thought you said you had plans tonight. Won't that be a little early for you to get up?"

Ugh. He's like the anti-mom, schooling me on

the proper art of partying. "I know how to go to a party, have fun, *and* get to bed at a reasonable hour, Hunter. Do you?"

"What party?"

"None of your business."

"I'm just being polite, Tass. Not like I'm going to crash it."

Whatever. "I'm meeting Rach at her sister's." Her older sister lives in downtown Houston and works at some talent agency. Rach has guaranteed bountiful man candy for our viewing pleasure as well as free frou-frou drinks and lots of girl talk. I'm not planning to drink since I'll be driving home late.

"Really now?" He sounds devilish.

"What's that supposed to mean?"

"Nothing," he says all too innocently.

"Didn't sound like nothing."

"I just happen to be going to Justine's party, too."

Justine is Rach's sister. "What? You said you weren't going to crash."

"I'm not. I know Justine from high school. She's trying to convince me to sign with her agency."

I completely forgot that he'd dated Justine. It was years ago. She was a senior, and he was a sophomore. That's how good-looking the son of a bitch is—he had seniors chasing after him.

"Well, great. Now you just completely ruined my night." *And tonight just happens to be my—wait. No. I don't celebrate today. It's against my rules.*

"I'm only going to meet the owner of the agency," he says. "They're getting into sports, and they've offered to represent me for half the commission of the other agencies."

I'm silent on the matter. He knows I don't want to see him there.

"If it makes you feel any better, I'll only stay for a few minutes and then I'll leave, though we could drive together if I stayed."

Nuh-uh. "No. We're *not* driving together. I don't know you. You don't know me. We'll be two invisible boats passing in the night. And our engines will be electric, so there's no noise."

"God, you're a strange woman."

"And this just occurred to you." I practically wear the strange flag on my forehead.

"I generally tend to notice your lips more than anything. And your wide blue eyes. Your smile is nice to look at, too." His voice is low and serious and instantly sparks an unwelcome reaction inside my stomach.

"See you in the morning." I end the call.

Damn this guy! How dare he start talking flirty-sexy to me. Now I'm feeling all flustered. He's sucked me in again. The man is an emotional black hole with gravitational forces beyond my control. I slam my fist down on the washer.

My mother suddenly appears. "Tassie? Everything okay?"

I nod with a clipped smile. "Yeah. Everything's fine." Just as soon as I blast this football monster from my life.

CHAPTER TWENTY

Tonight, I'm stepping out of my comfort zone and wearing my shortest outfit—a black dress I purchased weeks ago for my charade with Hunt, but I feel it fits the night. Short, sexy, fashionable for a woman like me who knows only two things about style: show some cleavage (aka my womanly speed bumps) and show those quasi-toned shaved legs. I've worn my hair all crazy—full-on blow-out—that will give the impression I've arrived on a motorcycle sans helmet. My lips are cherry red. My blue eyes are smoky. My black heels are tap-tap high, meaning I can't manage a step wider than a Chihuahua. *Tap, tap, tap.*

Yes. I'm a vision of nerdy hotness.

Why?

Hunter.

That conversation with him has lit a fire of pure frustration in my lady furnace, and I'm determined to bury him under a rubble of smokin' hot lovers. What better place to start than a party filled with hot male models dressed in blue jeans and cowboy hats?

I enter the penthouse suite through the private elevator and my first reaction is to cry. Like, blubber. Hard. I'm outgunned, outboobed, and outlegged. Blondes, brunettes, size zero goddesses encrust nearly every single inch of space in the stylish loft.

"Fuck. Me," I whisper. No one said that the women here would be twelves—on a scale of one to ten. That makes me a four at best, and a four might as well be invisible. No revenge lovers for me tonight.

"Tass!"

I look to my right and see Rach surrounded by a group of very beautiful people. She's wearing her red hair in a big bun and has on a silver sequin dress cut just above the pubic bone. Seriously, the hem is so high I can almost see her g-spot.

"Hey, Tass!" She gallops through the crowd and hugs me.

"I can't believe how much I've missed you." I hug her tightly and whisper in her ear, "But what the hell is up with these women?"

She growls. "I know, right?"

"You said there'd be hot guys here."

Her face explodes with guilty colors. "Oh, don't you worry, baby. They. Are. On. The way…"

I wrinkle my nose. "Really?"

"Real-ly." She nods exaggeratedly. "In fact, there's this one model you have to meet. I'm talkin' hot. Cover model. *Playgirl* material."

I nod. "I have no idea what that actually means." I've never picked up a *Playgirl* in my life.

She pinches my cheek. "Consider it my birthday present."

I glare at her. "You know that talking about my *today* is a sensitive subject." It is the reason that I have not thought about it once and instructed my parents many years ago to never celebrate it. Because I don't. My theory is that age is just a number and if you convince yourself you're getting older, then you will. It's a theory that will take a lifetime to prove out, but let's see if I still look twenty when I'm fifty. Then there is the whole idea of slowly decaying over time, which terrifies me. Anyway, everyone in my life is prohibited from mentioning *today*. Even me.

"Tassie, I don't think anybody cares how old you are. I mean, come on." She grabs a drink from a passing waiter with a tray and hands it to me. It's got some pink stuff in it.

"Well, I don't think; I *know* nobody cares." I sniff the drink. It smells like cotton candy and some very strong alcohol, so I hold it out for her to take.

She pushes it back to me. "Then?"

"Then nothing," I reply.

"Then happy birthday!"

"No," I growl. "You know I don't celebrate my *today*. Not since I was four."

"This year, yes, you do."

"No," I growl.

"Yes!" She points toward the elevators. "And there's your man candy now."

"What?"

"I decided you needed a little party fun to kick off the night. Happy birthday, Tassie!"

The elevator doors burst open and my lungs collapse. *Oh, dear Lord.* I shield my eyes. I can't believe she's tricked me.

"No…" I groan.

"Yes," she hisses.

Three incredibly built men in tight jeans burst from the elevator. Music, with deep base, explodes from the speakers in the room. The men are topless, ripped, and positively sexual.

"Um, wow…" is all I can manage to say.

"Over here!" Rach yells and points to me.

The three guys—one blond and two with brown hair—zero in on me and make their way over, forming a line right in the middle of the living room, directly in front of me. The stylishly dressed crowd, most sipping martinis and in their twenties, circles around us as the show begins. Manly hips thrust, abs flex, and bulgy arms bulge.

My body explodes with hot blushes. I've never been the center of attention in a way like this, and I can't help laughing. It's half nerves and half hysteria.

How could she do this to me? In front of a room full of strangers, no less. I suppose it's no worse than going to one of those bars, but I wouldn't be caught dead in one of those either.

The song ends, some dance thing I don't even recognize, and just when I think it's over, another song starts. "I Want Your Sex" by George Michael.

Rachel fans her face, and the women howl. I am giggling awkwardly, dying of embarrassment. Until the elevator doors open again.

Hunter.

His eyes are on me like anger on a dictator, like hunger on a tiger, like rage on a group of political protestors. For a moment, I feel embarrassed, but I'm not his. I never have been. Never will be. I can air-hump whomever I choose.

So I do.

The guy with brown hair in the middle struts up to me and bends at the knees, pumping his hips. I join in, meeting him thrust for thrust, eliciting ear-piercing shouts from everyone.

He stands up and grabs my arms and bends to my cheek. His tongue licks down the side of my neck, across my collarbone, to my breast bone.

It kind of feels good to be bad. It feels good to do something that doesn't involve grades or Hunter.

Only…

I feel the guy pull away and a rumble erupts from the crowd.

What the…

Hunter, who's dressed in a snug black button-down shirt and blue jeans, makes the time-out sign with his hands. "Shut that fucking music off."

No. No, you don't! "Don't you dare shut it off. I

was enjoying—"

The music dies, but the rumble of voices doesn't.

"What are you doing?" I seethe.

"We need to talk."

"No. You need to talk, which I agreed to let you do tomorrow morning so that we can finally put the past where it belongs."

"Well, what if I don't want to put us in the past?" His chest expands with panted, angry breaths.

"That's not your choice, Hunter."

"Maybe not, but I'm not about to let you make up your mind until you've at least heard me out."

"I heard plenty already, Mr. Bet. And in case you haven't noticed," I glance at the half-naked guy to my side, "I've already made up my mind. I've moved on."

"With a stripper?" Hunter snarls.

"No." I look at the guy. "Though I'm sure you're a very nice person, so no offense." The stripper guy shrugs, and I turn back to Hunter. "I'm moving on from you because you're an overgrown man-child looking for someone to sit on the sidelines and wave pompoms while you go onto the NFL. I'm a grown woman with a future ahead of her and you will never be part of that equation. So there is no discussion. There is no us. So why don't *you* go back to your silly frat games."

"You know what? *You* are demagogue!"

"I'm a...demagogue?"

His gorgeous face turns an angry red. "That's right. I know big words, too, Tass. And you are a fomenter! A radical, incendiary. An emotional terrorist."

God. Where does he get off using such expressive terms with me? Articulation makes me hot!

Whoa. Hold on. Maybe big words make me hot, but Hunter doesn't.

I nod and put my hands on my waist. "At least I didn't fornicate with you for points."

"Didn't you?" he snarls back.

"No." *He's lost it.*

"You made it clear you only used me for sex."

I can't believe we're having this conversation. Like I'm some manizing whore. "I am *not* the one who took that bloody T-shirt to show to your friends."

The party guests, who are probably enjoying the drama, make horrible sounds. Yes, I've crossed the TMI line. So what?

"I would never do that to you," he snaps back.

"Did you or did you not tell everyone you'd fuck me and provide proof?" I turn toward the crowd. "Oh yeah. That's right, people. Just like the good old days when they flew the bloody virginal sheet out the window." I point to Hunter. "That's the kind of guy he his."

"Hey, man," says the stripper guy with brown hair, "I think you should go."

Hunter turns with clenched fists. "This is between Tassie and me, so go mind your own fucking business."

Hunter is much bigger than Mr. Stripper and the last thing I want is two hotheads going at it. Besides, Hunter getting into trouble at this stage of his life could ruin everything.

And idiot me cares. What's the matter with me?

Still, I can't help myself. I step between the two, facing Hunter. "Oh. My. God. You've learned nothing, Hunter. Nothing at all. But I have. I don't want to see you again, and if it takes going to another college and never going home again, then that's what I'll do. But you. Are. Toxic. Wake up!" I throw my drink in his face.

I march from the party, taking the elevator and walking to my car, which is parked on the street.

Halfway home, I realize a car is behind me. It's been behind me for miles. Ten miles later, I see it's a red Mustang. Hunter.

Oh. Oh…now you're asking for it.

Twenty minutes later, my mind is made up. I'm going to kick the shit out of him. I'll jump on his shoulders and bite off his ears. I'll head butt that perfect nose of his. *I'm going to jail, baby!*

By the time I pull into my parents' driveway, I've realized how ridiculous that is. Violence doesn't resolve anything. And I really, really can't stand seeing it in any form. Freaks me out.

I get out of my car, knowing he's getting out of his, too.

"Tass! Get over here! We need to talk."

I ignore him and head for my front door, fumbling for the key.

"So that's it, huh? You're going to chuck me aside again. Just like that? Like you did when we were six?"

I pause with the key in my hand. "That's not true, Hunter."

"Isn't it?"

I turn and look at him standing on the walkway. "No. It's not."

"Then what do you call a girl who fucks with your head for over a decade and then when you put everything on the line for her, she refuses to look at you? What about that?"

I march down the steps, pointing in his face. "You fucked me for a bet. For fucking points, Hunter! You lied! To me!"

"I fucked you because I wanted to fuck you. The bet was just an excuse to grow some balls, because you're so damned impossible!"

"What! I am *not* impossible. I'm just stupid for trusting you!"

"Yes. You *are* stupid." His face riles in mine. "Who else would doubt a guy who almost went to jail to help her? Or who lied to his parents? We almost went bankrupt because of you, and you've never showed an ounce of gratitude."

"Because I didn't remember!"

"No! Because you're a judgmental snob like

your stuck-up parents. And you've never quite comprehended the fact that I've been in love with you since we were five! So...fuck you! And fuck your fam—"

"Hunter," a stern female voice barks to our side. It's his mother.

My eyes do a one-eighty sweep. *Oh, God.* My parents are standing behind me. His parents are standing to our side.

They heard everything. Including the bit about him fucking me.

I'm horrified.

"I had to pay one hundred thousand dollars because of *her*?" his father growls. He's a big man with big arms and a receding hairline.

"Hey!" my dad barks. "Watch your mouth."

"Why? My son almost went to prison. For this little stuck-up princess," Hunter's dad lobs back.

"Screw you, Mr. Johnson!" I roar. "You're nothing but a bully who picks on your family. You have no right!"

"Tassie!" my mother spits. "Don't talk to him that way, even if he is a Neanderthal."

"He's *not* a Neanderthal," Hunter snarls. "And he cares more about me than you've ever cared about Tassie. He gave up his retirement to keep me out of jail and you won't even give your own daughter the time of day because she's not in some fucking lame sorority."

"You!" my father interjects, pointing at Hunter.

"Don't you dare talk to my wife that way, or I'll—"

"You'll what?" Hunter's dad steps forward, and I realize this is about to turn into a fight.

"Stop!" screams Hunter's mother. "I've stayed quiet long enough." She points to Hunter's dad. "Get your head out of your ass. Hunter is our son, and he made his choices. So did we. You can't blame Tassie for any of it." She looks at my father. "And shame on you and your wife for always judging us. We almost lost our house. We almost lost everything. But would you so much as offer us a smile or a few kind words? No. Because you're too good for your own glasses. So...shame on you!"

And just as I'm about to speak, unsure of what I'll say, my mother steps off the porch, looking at her feet. "I am so sorry," she practically whispers. "Millie, I didn't know how you felt."

Hunter's mom's name is Millie.

"Well, now you do," Millie says.

Hunter's dad opens his mouth, but Millie silences him with a threatening finger. "Not another word, Gerald, or so help me I will leave you. I'm done with your pigheaded bullying."

Hunter's dad, Gerald, looks shocked. Not angry, but shocked. Like a child who's been given a time-out.

"Tassie?" says my father.

I look at him, having zero idea of what he's about to say.

"Millie is right." He shakes his head. "This situation isn't logical. And it has gone on long enough. I suggest you and Hunter decide."

"Decide what?" I ask.

My dad takes a deep breath, removes his glasses, and pinches the bridge of his nose. "We have always known that your relationship with Hunter is complicated. Any fool can see you two are obsessed with each other and always have been. But we didn't interfere because we believed you would work it out once you got older. We were wrong. You haven't worked it out, and things seem to have gotten more complicated. I think you need to decide if you're going to love him or forget him, but no more hate. No more fighting, honey. Look at the damage it's caused all of us."

My eyes tear. "Damage?" I whisper.

My dad wipes the stream of wetness from under my eyes. "There's nothing a parent won't do for their children, Tass. And that includes fighting with your neighbors because their son made you so sad."

Oh. So I guess my pretending that I was okay all these years didn't work. My parents saw right through me, which explains why our families never really got along.

I look at Hunter, who seems absolutely twisted inside. Then I look back at my dad and his glassy blue eyes.

"We love you, Tassie," says my dad. "And we are always in your corner, no matter what you do with your life. But we can't let you two ruin your lives. You're both too smart and full of so much potential. And you're holding each other back."

He's right. I know he is. All this drama has stolen energy from Hunter and me, energy we could've spent on other things.

"You have to decide now, sweetie," my dad says. "But our families aren't going to keep doing this. At least, I don't want to."

My dad looks at Hunter's father, who jerks his head and says, "How about a beer?"

My father doesn't drink beer. Only red wine for his heart health. Still, he smiles. "Love to."

"I'm in, too," my mom says.

They all walk away, talking quietly. Peace has been made in a war that Hunter and I started as children. I just never understood how deeply it had affected everyone.

I look up at Hunter, who's staring down with that tight jaw and those sensual lips pinched. He's so beautiful. And I realize he's no longer that little boy who used to pull my hair. He's all grown up. Really, really grown up. But deep down inside, maybe we still felt like those little kids who just didn't know how to deal with our feelings.

"So, the bet, huh?" I mutter.

He takes my hand. "It was inexcusable, but it was also just an excuse to go for it. I've wanted you for a very long time, Tass. I didn't lie about that."

"Oh." I feel like my heart might crumble.

"Oh?"

I shrug and look down.

"What does 'oh' mean, Tass?"

"It really hurt when I thought you used me just to win." I sigh. "And I want you, too."

He steps in close and rubs his thumb over my lower lip. "Stupid girl. I would never use you. I just wanted to be with you—the girl next door who crushed my heart in kindergarten. Also the girl who didn't put up with my bullshit and tormented me with her little laugh and little walk and her big words for the last decade."

My mind starts to deconstruct the thousands of memories I've stashed away inside my head of Hunter and me. I think I chose to remember the bad stuff, the teasing and torment, but there were times when he did try—buying me chocolates on Valentine's or giving me a big box of funny elf pencils for Christmas. He even invited me out a few times to eat, but I never took him seriously. I just chalked it all up to him trying to play a prank. "Sorry. Not falling for whatever frolicsomeness you've envisioned in your cranium, Hunter." Or, "Sorry, Hunter. But my intelligence can only be spent on matter—which you don't."

I suppose I could see why Hunter might need a hard push to go for it when I'd shot him down so many times. His argument, that the bet gave him an excuse to be with me, makes sense, I suppose.

The waterworks start up again, and I wipe the tears away. "Dammit. See what you did?" I sob my words.

"What, Tassie?"

"You made me not be mad at you anymore," I cry. "How do you do that to me?"

He pulls me into his broad chest and plants a kiss on the top of my head. "Because you secretly love me?"

I sink into his strong frame and inhale his sweet scent. Love. Now there's a word I never thought I'd associate with Hunter. And he's right, my feelings run deep. Otherwise, he wouldn't get to me like he does. "Clearly I'm into you," I sniffle.

"I'm into you, too. Ever since you convinced me that I was destined for great things and to never give up."

I pull back and look up at those hypnotic blue eyes. "I said that?"

He nods. "Yes. You were studying Latin root words at the time. You told me that Hunter means greatness. You were five, but you were very convincing."

My mind can't. It just can't. But it has to. Everything in my world—planets, stars, and the microcosms inside my cells—have finally aligned. For once in my life, it all feels so right.

"Will you please kiss me now?" I ask.

He grins, full dimples and everything. "Yes. Yes, I will. If you will be my real girlfriend and go out on a date with me. No more pretending."

"I'd like that."

He dips his head and kisses me with soft, warm lips. I realize that this is the kiss I've been waiting for my whole life. And it's better than anything I could've imagined.

CHAPTER TWENTY-ONE

The rest of Thanksgiving week is a blur of emotions—me and Hunter, our families, and dealing with letting go of a reality that no longer exists. That's the funny thing about facing the truth, it's hard to swallow, but it also sets you free. My new reality is helping me see possibilities and the future. One that will be with Hunter. Turns out, he is going pro. After college. He says that he only plans to play for a few years and then wants to go into teaching. Science of all things. My heart fucking melted right then and there.

"I always knew you were a closet smarty, Hunter. I'm so hot for you right now." Seriously, imagining him teaching, expanding minds? So, so sexy.

"You always were a sucker for education," he replied with that cocky little smile.

Anyway, Hunter and I have been going crazy for alone time all week, but we haven't had a moment of privacy since the big family showdown.

That night, my brother arrived and I had to

spend quality time with him, catching up. The next night, Hunter's parents came over for fondue. It was actually pretty funny because our dads discovered they're both into birds. Yeah. Birds. My dad has a couple of feeders in the yard and uses a program to track them as part of a subroutine that correlates bird migration to weather patterns. And Hunter's dad…well, he likes to shoot birds and eat them. Not exactly the same thing, but it's common ground and a good place to start a new relationship.

Then the following day, Rach and I went for our girls' day out. Toes. Manicures. Facials. And lots of talk about her new guy—some botanist she met at school. Yes, they slept together, so she and I got to compare notes. For scientific purposes, of course.

The week flew by, but there wasn't a moment that I wasn't pining for Hunter. Those lips. That body. His sweet smile and voice. But more importantly, I craved our connection. It existed at a level so deep that my heart pattered with the thought of holding his hand. My body, on the other hand, exploded at the thought of being alone again. Skin on skin. Heart to heart. Breath with breath.

Thanksgiving Thursday, after we have dinner with our families, Hunter and I meet outside. "Let's go home tomorrow," he says, kissing me, panting, pushing into me as we stand on his porch. I feel like dragging him into the bushes and having my way with him.

"Tomorrow?" I kiss him hard. "My mother will

be upset if I leave early."

"I will be more upset if we're not alone, Tassie." He nuzzles my neck. "I can't wait any more. I need to be with you."

That's the other truth I came to fully understand this week. Hunter told me more about how mean I was to him when we were little. He'd try to talk to me, but I'd only roll my eyes or tell him he wasn't as smart as me. Honestly, now looking back, I really was a huge heartless demagogue. It makes sense that he bit back. Underneath it all, however, I feel like we didn't let it go because we preferred to have a bad relationship than no relationship at all. Then we got smart and grew the hell up.

Hunter suddenly looks at me and sticks out his lower lip, making it quiver. His blue eyes go all round and saucerlike. "Paweez, Tassie?"

"Oh, hell. Not the puppy face. You know what that does to me." I can't help cracking up.

Hunter keeps it up.

"Okay," I say. "Let's leave at six a.m.? That'll give us almost three whole days before Elle or your roommates come back."

He kisses me again, gripping me tightly with his strong hands. "It's not enough, but I'll take it."

So will I. And I think this weekend is a good time to tell him that I've thought it over and have decided that I definitely exhibit the classic signs of being in love. Heart patters, inability to imagine a future where he's not in it, and an insatiable urge to make him mine forever. Plus sex. I really want to fuck him again. Like dirty, nasty, animal sex. Yup.

He deepens the kiss, making me want so much more. I don't know how I'll ever be able to get through classes now. I'll only be thinking of him.

"Tassie!" screams a tiny sobbing voice.

Both Hunter and I turn to see Elle coming from her Nissan.

"Elle?" I let go of Hunter and rush over to meet her. "What happened?" I know it has to be bad, and it has to be her mother. Why else would she be here?

"I can't do it anymore, Tassie." She throws her arms around me and sobs. "I can't." She drops to her knees, and I hold her but look up at Hunter, who's completely lost. He doesn't have a clue what to do either.

I stroke the back of her head. "What happened, Elle? Tell me?"

She just cries in my arms.

TO BE CONTINUED...

AUTHOR'S RAMBLE

Hey There!

I hope you enjoyed the story. If yes, I've got more coming soon. SIGN UP HERE (https://goo.gl/9NZiqR) for new release alerts and exciting tips on dusting or stain removal. (Okay. A complete lie. I know nothing about stains and only dust before my mom and dad come to visit.)

As for you SWAG lovers, I've got free signed bookmarks as always (first come basis). Don't forget to mention if you posted a review (aka "showed the book love!"). I have awesome magnets as thank yous for those who do. (Also first come basis, so hurry!)

As for The Ohellno Series, Elle and Henry come next!

OH, HENRY
Book #2, The OHELLNO Series

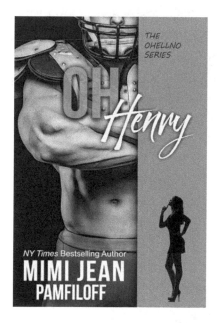

Henry Walton has been called many things throughout his life—fatty, bathtub, tree trunk, moose, walrus, lardo—you name it. But at over six foot five and weighing two hundred and eighty pounds, Henry is now solid muscle and the hottest defensive end in the NFL college draft. This is the moment he's been waiting for: fame, money, women, and glory. Okay, there's also a ten-million-dollar contract in it for him.

There's just one teeny tiny problem: He can't quite get over being dumped by the coldhearted shrew with thick glasses and a genius IQ he dated for a mere few weeks. Elle.

God, he so hates her and that stupid little squeaky laugh—a laugh that sounds like music to his ears and sweet, sweet victory to his career. Because for those two perfect weeks, his game was perfect. And now that she refuses to talk to him, everything is falling down the crapper.

Call him superstitious, but he's got to get her back. Even if she's the last girl he really wants and she hates his guts.

SIGN UP for an alert when this book goes on sale.

In any case, I hope you enjoyed the story. I will tell you this: while I never dated a football player, I certainly hated them. High school jocks definitely left a mark on me—*they're idiots!* But later in life, as I began to confront more and more of my biases, everything I detested was up for hole-poking.

Anyway, this book comes from my heart. A statement about what makes us all worth our weight in gold: The willingness to love those who are different than ourselves.

But it's not enough to feel it; we have to take steps to reach out and show what's in our hearts. Because, and trust me on this, they don't know. The people we're separated from, who live in worlds different than our own, they don't know we're here caring unless we show them.

Every opportunity you get to reach out—one human being to another—is an opportunity for you to change the landscape of this world.

In closing, I'll tell you that had I not taken off my blinders, I would not have found the love of my life and married him.

Love,
Mimi

MIMI'S PLAY LIST

(Yup! These are the tunes I wrote the story to if you enjoy a little mood music with your books like I do!)

"Young Blood" by Bea Miller
"Riptide" by Vance Joy
"Heart It Races" by Dr. Dog
"Like I'm Gonna Lose You" by Jasmine Thompson
"Dream" by Priscilla Ahn
"I'll Keep You Safe" by Sleeping At Last
"Running Back to You" (feat. Allison Weiss) by For
    The Foxes
"Peaches" by In The Valley Below
"Roses" (feat. Rozes) by The Chainsmokers
"40 Day Dream" by Edward Sharpe & The
    Magnetic Zeros
"I Turn My Camera On" by Spoon
"Someone New" by Hozier
"Dug My Heart" by Børns
"Hang Me Up to Dry" by Cold War Kids
"Fire And The Flood" by Vance Joy
"Help I'm Alive" by Metric
"Gold Guns Girls" by Metric
"Blindness" by Metric
"Beautiful Thing" by Grace VanderWaal

ACKNOWLEDGEMENTS

A big OH HELL YEAH! to all the folks who stepped up to the plate and took time out of their busy days to read and provide word coaching (sports talk!): Kylie, Dalitza, Ally, and Naughty Nana. Another cheer goes out to Sarah and Ashlee for using their young brains to sanity check the opening chapter.

And, as always, my gratitude goes out to the wonderful professionals who help get this book all shiny and sparkly for the world: Latoya, Pauline, Su (looooove this cover, woman!) and Paul.

Thank you!
Mimi

COMING SOON!

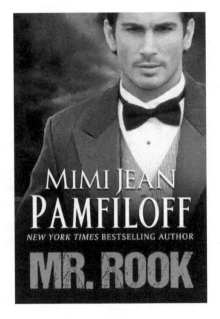

Sail the high seas with a dashingly wicked pirate.
Be swept off your feet by a ruggedly
handsome cowboy.
Hike through a dangerous jungle in search of
ancient treasures.

**AT ROOK'S ISLAND, YOUR FANTASY IS
OUR BUSINESS…**

Located near the Bermuda Triangle, some believe that Mr. Rook's Island is an urban legend. However, their exclusive clientele will say it's a paradise worth every penny. Because for a small fortune, they'll make your wildest fantasies come to life.

But Stephanie Fitzgerald doesn't care about fairytales or romantic picnics. She only wants to find her sister, who never returned from her exotic vacation.

To get answers, Stephanie will have to impersonate a guest and get close to the island's mysterious owner, the handsome Mr. Rook. But he's not about to give away the island's secrets. And Stephanie is about to discover that paradise has a dark side.

GO TO: www.mimijean.net/rooksIsland.html

ABOUT THE AUTHOR

San Francisco native MIMI JEAN PAMFILOFF is a *USA Today* and *New York Times* bestselling romance author. Although she obtained her MBA and worked for more than fifteen years in the corporate world, she believes that it's never too late to come out of the romance closet and follow your dream. Mimi lives with her Latin lover hubby, two pirates-in-training (their boys), and the rat terrier duo, Snowflake and Mini Me, in Arizona. She hopes to make you laugh when you need it most and continues to pray daily that leather pants will make a big comeback for men.

Sign up for Mimi's mailing list for giveaways and new release news!